SHADOW MASQUE

SHADOW MASQUE

IRIS COMFORT

DOUBLEDAY & COMPANY, INC.

GARDEN CITY, NEW YORK

1980

All of the characters in this book
are fictitious, and any resemblance
to actual persons, living or dead,
is purely coincidental.

First Edition

ISBN: 0-385-17088-2
Library of Congress Catalog Card Number: 80–495
Copyright © 1980 by Iris Comfort
All Rights Reserved
Printed in the United States of America

SHADOW MASQUE

CHAPTER 1

Petrina Gentry shivered and pulled her raincoat tighter around her, huddling back into the entry stoop of the shabby doll shop. She looked ruefully at the once crisp morning newspaper she pulled from under her arm. Instead of snapping, the paper unfolded limply when she shook it out to make herself a protective hood.

On an inner page was the interview she'd given a young reporter yesterday and a three-column picture of her holding Peter, along with a nice dark cut-line that started,

"Young American ventriloquist Petrina Gentry follows in her father's footsteps to become a hit at the Berwyck—"

So much for fame. At least she would have a presentable hairdo when David arrived. If he got there before the newspaper gave out.

Blast him, anyhow. He knew she was due back at the theater at eleven so the stage manager could go over cues with her for a new bit of business she had added to her routine. She had told David about the appointment last night.

Thin mist slicked the dingy reaches of London's Pengable Street and turned early morning headlights into wavering tracks on the wet pavement. The newspaper was getting soggy and she pressed against the ancient rotting boards that framed the heavy door and gave off a dank smell of decay in the humid air.

She tried to see through the dust-streaked windows but

grime totally obscured the shop's interior. Only the battered sign over the door, lettered almost illegibly DOLLS, gave any indication of what merchandise might be encountered within.

David had better hurry if he expected her to wait for him and see the antique ventriloquist's doll he had checked out yesterday.

The door pushed open against her and a heavy-set workman stared at her with hard eyes until she stepped aside and left him enough room to get out onto the pavement. Head ducked down into his turned-up collar, he grunted a surly "Ta!" and hurried off.

The door swung shut again blocking her view of the dim interior but not before she'd glimpsed a knot of men gathered around the counter near a cash register. Very odd. She'd been waiting out front at least half an hour for David and in that length of time no one had entered the shop, not by the front entrance anyhow. A doll shop was a peculiar gathering spot for a group of men in rough working clothes.

Strange that Morag would have pointed out this place to David, especially when she must have known his interest would have been because of Petrina. An Irish dancer like Morag, Petrina thought, a famous American mentalist like David Nairac and a struggling American ventriloquist like herself—three more unlikely people could hardly have been found to have an interest in a seedy doll shop in this out-of-the-way neighborhood. Sardonic, fastidious David must have cut quite a figure down here yesterday.

The building didn't stop the wind and she was becoming chilled. She thrust her hands deeper into her pockets and her fingers accidentally brushed across the crumpled cable jammed there before she had left the hotel this morning. She jerked her hand away hurriedly. If the desk clerk hadn't been watching her after she opened the envelope, she would have tossed the message away unread. But she'd read it and pocketed it and now it was too late. Linette must have finagled her address from her agent in New York.

David's small black car darted suddenly out of the stream of traffic like a frantic wet water beetle and with a last bat of its windshield wipers halted at the curb. The door flew open and he sprang out, his narrow dark face tightened by tension lines that eased when he saw her in the entry.

"I got held up, Trina. Sorry I'm late." With two loping strides he was across the sidewalk and hurrying her along. "Let's go, luv. This is not the morning to dally."

For a moment she was outraged and then she caught the teasing glint of amusement flickering across his dark eyes.

"On the way back to your theater I'll tell you what happened to me," he promised.

As they entered the dingy shop she glanced about curiously. From shelves reaching up toward a cracked ceiling stared row upon row of dolls, some rare and valuable, some battered and desperately in need of repair, their features blurred with accumulated dirt.

The workmen she had seen earlier were now exiting rapidly through a rear doorway. Around their flushed and angry faces hung unheard echoes of argument though not a word was being spoken by any one of them.

A spare form, startlingly devoid of padding flesh, detached itself from the shadows near a back corner of the shop and came forward, ignoring the departing group.

"Mr. Nairac!" He smiled stiffly, a drawing of tight facial skin back to bare his teeth. "You did come back! I'm glad you got here. Is this the young lady who might be interested in the Colonel?" His eyes sharpened and he leaned closer, studying her face in the dim light. "Yes, of course. Now I understand. The young American ventriloquist who opened at the Berwyck last week! I hear you are doing very well, Miss Gentry. Very well, indeed. But not at all surprising, either, is it? Talent and beauty are quite a formidable combination."

"Thank you." Petrina's dry acknowledgment did not encourage additional blandishments.

"We are pressed for time, Mr. Conolly." David looked about impatiently.

"Yes, Mr. Nairac." Without further delay the shopkeeper lifted a tall uniformed doll from its seat on a stool against the wall and held the puppet in a standing position on the top of the counter.

"The Colonel is a very old gentleman," Mr. Conolly said. "He came into my possession at an auction, along with a trunk of various costumes and a thick logbook telling of his various travels and appearances through the late eighteen hundreds and early nineteen hundreds. He has traveled all over the world, the Colonel, and he has the playbills to prove it."

Petrina took the doll in her arms, wrinkling her nose against the musty smell that rose from his wig as she smoothed it. She slipped her hand carefully through the opening in his back and checked his head suspension and lever attachments with quick movements of her fingers. He would not need a great deal of work to make him agile, and after a good airing—

David chuckled. "The lady will take the Colonel, Mr. Conolly. At the price we agreed upon yesterday."

"Too bad I didn't wait to set a price," Mr. Conolly remarked regretfully. "I could have gotten twice as much from the lady herself, I suspect. I never learn."

The shopkeeper packed the doll away in a small worn

trunk with the logbook wedged against one end and waited as Petrina counted out the thirty-eight-pound purchase price for him. "Good luck to you, Miss Gentry." Mr. Conolly latched the trunk. "I hope to hear that the Colonel has joined your act in future."

Petrina moved to get a better look through the smeared glass of the counter at two fine old Pedlar dolls, improbably half-buried by surrounding trash. "I've started a doll collection," she confided. "What are you asking for the doll on the left? With the tray full of baubles?"

"They both have trays full of baubles," David laughed. "You can't take time for more shopping this morning, Trina. We'll have to come back tomorrow." He turned to Mr. Conolly. "Put the doll on the left away for her, Mr. Conolly, and we'll look at it tomorrow. I do think you've made another sale."

He picked up the shabby case and carried it out to his car, stowed it away in the trunk. After they had gotten in and the car was moving down Pengable Street toward Linden, he glanced over at her.

"What's bothering you, Trina?" he asked. "Have you heard from Linette?"

She turned her face away to hide her quick flush. "How did you know? Did our agent tell you?"

"Ken telephoned me from New York about a week ago and told me she had called him for your address. He wondered if he should give it to her. I said I didn't think it could do any harm—now. So she got around to communicating, did she?"

"You had no right!" She was so angry that her voice shook. "You knew that I didn't want to hear from her or Tony ever again! You, of all people, know what they did to me!"

His hand came down over hers and she tried to harden herself against the persuasion of his touch. "What did she want?" he asked.

She noticed the way he had couched his question. He hadn't asked *if* Linette had wanted something. There was no need. Linette would not have gotten in touch if she hadn't wanted something and he knew it.

"She cabled that she needs me desperately, to come home at once."

"You'll have to telephone her and find out what this is about, of course. She is your cousin, Trina, the only family you have left. I'll drive you to the theater first so you can attend to your business with the stage manager and afterward we'll have lunch and then you can call Cypress Glade. If you like, I will place the call for you in case Tony answers the phone."

"Maybe neither one of them will be home." Her voice was wispy.

"Maybe. But that isn't very likely. It will be five hours earlier in Florida instead of six now that Daylight Savings Time has begun there. Besides, if we don't find her at home we can always call her lawyer and ask him what's going on. What is his name?"

The need to answer shook her to attention. "Sam Brock." She regarded him reproachfully. "You knew that."

"Certainly I did." He glanced over at her. "Feel better now?"

"A little." It was true.

"We're meeting Julian Farr for lunch, Trina. Remember I told you I have an English relative. He's been off on an assignment in Belfast and he's just returned. When he's in London he works for Scotland Yard on the anti-terrorist squad."

"And that was why you were late."

"That was why." He tucked her into his wet black car and sent it rushing to join the fast traffic, rocketing the long miles toward Piccadilly.

Her business with the stage manager took only a few minutes, in the end. He was in his office where he went over the cue sheet listing changes necessary and approved each one. There weren't that many.

"Where are we meeting Julian?" Petrina asked when she rejoined David out in the theater parking area.

"Petite Maison. It isn't far. I take it everything went well with your changes?"

Someone else might have asked to be polite. David really wanted to know. She glanced at him as she began to comb her satiny brown hair smooth and repair her makeup.

"Everything was fine. No problems." She thought of how many of her problems David had solved in the year she had known him. Problems were just about all she had when David had caught her act in that second-rate nightclub in Miami Beach and had coached her and helped her put together a really good routine. He and his agent had coerced friends into trying her out for a few months and they had gotten her booked on the talk shows that mattered. When David went to London himself as a headliner, they had even managed to get her booked at the Berwyck, not too far away. Around the middle of the bill, too, not trailing along at the end.

"It was a lucky day when you felt sorry for me and picked me up and set me on my feet," she told him.

She felt his eyes on her briefly. "Is that the way it was?" he asked.

"Well, wasn't it?"

His attention was back on the road. "If you say so." A faint smile curved his lips.

"I suppose I should even be glad Tony dropped me to

marry Linette," she said slowly. "No matter how much it hurt. It would never have worked." Her hazel eyes went bleak. "You don't think she's trying to reach me because of Tony! That she's having trouble with him. She couldn't possibly look to me for help!"

She could hear the naked bitterness in her voice and she was aware that David disliked it, but receiving that cable directly from Linette had bared too many of her buried feelings. David's face was impassive. "I'll place the call to Cypress Glade as soon as we get to the restaurant, if you want me to. I know the owner, Alex Varraux. We'll have no difficulty."

Varraux's office was quiet and the telephone available. By good luck circuits were open in the transatlantic stage as well as in the States to Cypress Glade.

"No answer." David held the instrument against his ear as though patience in listening to the mechanical ringing device might somehow help to produce a voice at the other end of the connection. At last he hung up. "I'll try for Sam Brock now." He waited long enough to give her a chance to argue if she wanted to and, when she didn't, went ahead with the call. There was no answer at Sam Brock's number, either. "We'll try again later." He frowned thoughtfully as he opened the office door for her.

The main dining area of the popular restaurant was crowded, but they were shown promptly to an ample table set back against the wall, ideally suited for privacy as well as a good view of the room.

"We may as well go ahead and order." David studied his menu. "Julian will be along any minute and you do have to get back to the theater for your matinee."

"Right." She made her selections quickly. "*Quiche de langouste.* And a light salad. *Mousse au chocolat.*"

"Inspired lady." David signaled the waiter. "I'll have lobster quiche, too. Salad and *mousse*. Martini, Trina?"

They sipped their drinks, but luncheon had been served and they had eaten and were almost ready for their coffee and Julian Farr still had not appeared.

"Telephone call for you, Mr. Nairac," their waiter interrupted quietly at David's elbow. "You can take it in M'sieur Varraux's office and he suggests that you do so."

David reappeared soon. His tall frame pushed through a cluster of waiters off toward the service door and as she saw the preoccupation that tightened his face, she came to her feet and hurried to meet him.

"Julian won't be able to get here." He settled accounts hurriedly with their waiter and swept her on into the foyer. "I won't be able to take you to the theater, Trina. I'll have to put you in a cab. But don't worry about your call to Florida. I'll get in touch with you later this afternoon and we'll get back to it."

As a cab pulled up to a stand in front of the restaurant, she saw his detachment change to acute awareness of her. "I would much rather that you didn't need to reach Linette, too," he admitted. "But that isn't the way it is, is it? Things have to be resolved, one way or another." He was closing the cab door when he remembered the Colonel. "I'll drop your new partner off at your hotel later today."

CHAPTER 2

The streets were still wet as Petrina's cab rushed toward the theater but the clouds were thinning overhead and the rain had turned to mist. They should have a pretty fair house this afternoon.

She joined the bustle and repartee of other arriving performers and dashed up to her dressing room. Katy had already pressed her three costumes and hung them carefully on their rack alongside the big makeup mirror. For still another time she thought how marvelous it was to be working in this British hall, with its convenient dressing rooms up on the second floor and its elevators down to the stage so traffic never jammed up. But most of all she luxuriated in a perk like Katy, her own dressing room maid, supplied by the management to take care of her costumes and help her dress, even to help with costume changes down on stage.

Katy came from around a screen to help her peel off street clothes and get into her first costume, the Spanish. Peter, her ventriloquist's doll, inherited from her father, already sat in his Spanish costume on a chair in the corner, his cheerful face curved in a challenging smile.

"You look good for your age, old fellow," she called to him, as though his beautifully fashioned ears might hear.

He had turned fifteen this year, an easy age to remember since she had been with her father in his dressing room in Chicago the day Peter was delivered. A friend of her father's, a fine old wood-worker, had fashioned him. She had looked at brand-new Peter, her eyes wide with five-year-old wonder, because the doll had her face, but also male brashness and aggressiveness. She had never found out if her father had meant to call him something else. She had named him Peter.

Petrina stripped off her street makeup and began to layer on her stage face. As always, she had a strange feeling as she watched the outlines of her delicate elfin street face change under her knowing fingers to an aloof seductive face that was surprisingly part of herself and yet alien and quite separate, too.

Years ago her father had told her that there was a precious chameleon quality about her that was as valuable as anything he might be able to teach her. That, from the great Robert Gentry, was the highest of compliments.

They hadn't given her his old dressing room, though, here at the Berwyck where he had played in triumph in his time. She hadn't earned that honor yet. But someday she would be good enough to play the top of the bill . . .

She smiled into the brightly lighted mirror.

"Kiss me, Katy!" she ordered in Peter's voice, using his Pedro accent.

Katy whirled and glared at the doll reprovingly. "Shame on you!" She burst into laughter. "You did it to me again, miss! That little monster has a life of his own, so help me!"

"Just as long as you're a believer, he has!" Petrina stood up so Katy could fasten her costume from behind. The Spanish costume fit her slight figure perfectly, giving her height, accenting her gentle curves into an oddly voluptuous fullness. She drew the wig with its tall Spanish comb thrust through black glossy curls from its stand. Carefully she eased it onto her own soft brown hair and sat down again so Katy could comb and fluff the hairpiece.

"Miss—"

Something about Katy's diffident yet determined overture alerted Petrina. "Something the matter, Katy?"

Her maid flushed with embarrassment. "Maybe it's nothing, miss, but I just thought you should know. Morag O Cathan, the Irish lady that dances with Ben Downey and is so interested in Mr. Nairac, she was in here earlier. She stayed for a bit, didn't take anything—I didn't move from the spot myself—but I had a feeling she had something on her mind more than she was saying. She said there was going to be a party at her flat after the show tonight and you were invited, and maybe you could bring Mr. Nairac with you."

"That's funny." Petrina glanced into the mirror and saw Katy nod vigorously.

"Indeed it did seem so," Katy agreed.

"We aren't friends," Petrina said slowly. "I wonder why she'd invite me to a party."

"I doubt it was she wanted to make a friend of you," Katy said tartly. "More likely she wants something or needs something."

"For that she'll have to stand in line, these days." Petrina went on with her makeup.

But Katy wasn't finished. "There's something I didn't like at all," she went on sturdily. "I told her so, too. She was picking up things at your dressing table, looking at your makeup, combing out your hairbrush. I asked her to take herself off and I'd give you the message. If she complains to you, that's what the truth of it is."

"You ran her off?" Petrina's eyes were admiring.

"You could say that, miss," Katy confirmed smugly. "Yes, you could say that."

The buzzer signaled that Petrina's entrance was coming up. She checked herself one more time.

Katy gathered up carefully the remaining two changes each for Petrina and Peter, one French with gamin-cut wigs to go with them, the other English with blond wigs. She glanced over at the doll.

"Pity he can't march himself down there instead of bothering us to get him there," she sniffed.

Petrina slipped her hand inside the doll's body and moved his levers, checked his head suspension, moved his eyes, lips. She did it automatically as she had given her own wig a last pat. In a way it was all part of a ritual before entering the arena.

"You can't have everything, Katy, *querida*," Peter said in his Spanish accent.

"Nervy little bit of firewood," Katy retorted, following along behind Petrina with her armload of costume changes to the waiting elevator that took them down to stage level.

Petrina was still reviewing changed cues in her mind as they reached the busy wing area of the stage. Morag O Cathan and Ben Downey were just finishing their turn, a strange wild folk dance done to a skirl of Irish bags and flute. Petrina stood back as they left the stage and found herself facing Morag, who stopped abruptly and reached out a slender finger to touch Petrina's cheek with a gesture more mocking than fond.

"You're coming tonight, aren't you?" she asked cajolingly. "You and David? Do bring your new doll with you so we can all see it!"

She was gone like a wisp of smoke, reappearing back at the control panel, where she engaged in animated conversation with the man on the switchboard.

Petrina took her position onstage while a stand-up comedian did his routine in front of the closed curtain. Bring the Colonel? Morag had told David originally that she had seen the Colonel in the doll shop, of course, but the grapevine was working unusually efficiently tonight to have the news of the sale out already.

A clatter of applause punctuated the end of the comedian's turn.

With a soft whisper of heavy crimson velvet, the stage curtains parted swiftly. Petrina lifted her face to the gold beam of the spotlight.

The white bench beneath her was almost hidden by the wide skirts of her Andalusian gown. Peter, on her knee in his Spanish costume, was called Pedro for this scene. She flexed her hand in his body.

She caught up her elaborate bright skirt with her other slim hand and moved lightly toward center stage as the footlights dimmed. From the cinema projectionist's booth a long finger of light pointed downward suddenly alongside the spot beam, focusing on the screen curtain at the back of the stage. Against the filmed brilliance of an Andalusian Romería del Rocio festival scene Petrina danced along with her puppet, making her way past filmed olive groves and roads crowded with wagons garlanded with flowers and streamers, men on horseback, laughing Spanish women.

From the sound track burst an exhilarating blend of singing guitars, castanets. It was a complicated illusion, blending the scene on the screen with the live woman and her puppet, and it depended critically on timing and precise cuing.

The first change in cuing came and went smoothly.

The second would occur during the French sequence, when she and Peter changed into the Apache costumes and Peter became Pierre. She dashed behind a stage screen where she made her own and Peter's change into the Apache costumes with Katy's help. As usual, Katy would stay behind the screen until the costume changes for the third and last sketch, the English.

The cue change for the French sequence was rough. The change for the English scene was close to disastrous.

Actually the audience was not aware of difficulty, but if Petrina had not been able to improvise dialogue for both herself and Peter to cover an unplanned-for music cut, the mistake would have been not only obvious but ridiculous. She was shaking with reaction as she took her bows. As she moved off to the wings she could see Katy's lips moving furiously as she gathered up the costumes and the curtain came down.

Petrina made way for the next turn, a flamboyant acrobatic team from Mexico, and glanced over toward the control panel. The man she had arranged her changes with earlier was not there now. A stranger was seated there. Against one of the flats she could see the momentary reflection of light off a silvery skirt like the one Morag wore, but in the blink of an eye it was gone. It might have been an optical illusion, too. What on earth had happened?

The elevator was clear and a few seconds later she emerged up into the dressing room corridor and opened the door to her own room.

Katy was giving a last pat to the costumes she had hung away in the closet. She turned and her deft fingers quickly unzipped Petrina's English ball gown and as Petrina stepped out of it, whisked it onto a hanger and away into the closet.

"What went wrong out there, miss?" Katy's face was still flushed. No one had to tell her there had been trouble.

"I don't know. The changes were so simple and the stage manager okayed them—and then something hap-

pened. They didn't follow them correctly." Petrina
scooped Peter up from her dressing table bench and
folded him in upon himself so he would fit into his carrying case. His expression as he looked up at her was mis-
chievous and faintly ribald, nestled against protective
padding. Peter was still every inch her father's partner.
The old wood-worker had given him Petrina's features
but he had also carved into that face her father's irrepres-
sible and irreverent nature.

"I'm going to send for a board and iron and give these
dresses a bit of a press," Katy frowned. "Maybe check the
seams and hems, too."

"I have a little repair work to attend to myself. Or
demolition might be more like it!"

As it turned out, she had no trouble finding the stage
manager. He was standing in front of the stage-level elevators almost as though he had been waiting for her.

"Miss Gentry, I heard what happened during your turn
and I can only tell you that you can be sure it won't
occur again. There was no excuse for Eddie to leave his
switchboard and we're still trying to find out who called
him to the telephone at just that time with an emergency
message of family disaster. If it was somebody's idea of a
prank, it certainly was a poor one. I apologize for all of
us."

"Then there was nothing wrong with the changes
themselves? Nothing to confuse the man at the board?"

"Nothing. Not to worry. It won't happen like that
again, you can depend on it."

With a sigh of relief Petrina thanked him and let herself out onto the late afternoon gloom of Argyll Street,
wet and chill in the continuing drizzle.

She stiffened as she saw Morag at the curb but it was
too late to avoid meeting her again. A tall black cab
pulled out of traffic and jerked to a stop and Morag

turned just as she was about to step inside, caught sight
of Petrina.

"This is great luck." There was no lilt in Morag's
brogue, only a peculiar satisfaction. "We can share the
ride! I'm on my way to Selfridge's and I can drop you off
at your hotel, if you like."

Petrina accepted reluctantly, unable to come up with a
satisfactory excuse quickly enough. She didn't want to
ride with Morag. And she was quite sure the Irish girl realized that fact and was amused by her discomfort, in-
terpreting it as jealousy of Morag's extravagant overtures
toward David.

"Have you thought over my invitation?" Morag asked.

"I haven't had a chance," Petrina answered truthfully.

"No, I don't suppose you have." Morag's lips curved
and her pale eyes glinted. "I heard about what happened
this afternoon. Too bad, but those things do happen,
don't they?"

"Do they?" Petrina regarded Morag carefully, wondering just how much Morag might have had to do with
what happened. What had she been doing at the control
panel after her act was over, anyhow?

Morag's pale eyes went as opaque as marbles. "Yes,
they do happen, and there's not much anybody can do
about it, either. But it's done with. No use stirring the
empty pot, is there?"

She was right about that. "Thanks for telling David
about the Colonel," Petrina said politely.

"If you really want to thank me, come tonight and
bring David, and anyone else you might want to include.
The more the merrier."

When the cab pulled up at Petrina's hotel, she insisted
on paying for her ride in spite of Morag's protest. She
was determined to be under no obligation at all to
Morag.

"I'll look for you," Morag said.

"I can't let you know until I have talked with David," Petrina temporized.

Morag's eyes were mocking. "You can tell me what David says tonight."

There was no message from David at the room clerk's desk nor had he left the trunk containing the Colonel for her. She went on up to her room, showered, slipped on her dressing gown and decided to nap for a while, setting the alarm for six o'clock.

At five-thirty the telephone rang, awakening her, as David called from the lobby. "I have the Colonel down here," he informed her urbanely. "If you're receiving, I'll bring him up. I can't stay so I won't delay you with conversation."

She was not at all surprised when the first thing he did after he came through the door was to deposit the Colonel's trunk on the floor near her desk and pick up the telephone. He grinned at her flouncy Victorian dressing gown. "Very fetching," he complimented. "Most becoming."

He placed the call to Linette in Cypress Glade again, and again there was no answer. "Now we try for Sam Brock. It will be a bit after twelve-thirty and we'll probably find the good man has just gone to lunch but we may as well give it a shot."

The phone rang quite a while, then he nodded triumphantly at her and began to talk. "I'm glad I was able to reach you, sir. Petrina received a cable from her cousin begging that she return home at once because she was needed desperately. She has tried to reach her cousin's house by phone and received no answer. Do you know why that message might have been sent?"

He listened intently, asking few questions. As the conversation ended, he shook his head slightly at Petrina to indicate there was no point in her speaking to Mr. Brock at that time. Puzzled and apprehensive, she was relieved that he was handling the matter. At last he said, "If you hear anything, please telephone at once or cable." He gave both their hotel addresses and the theater telephone numbers, too.

Laying the instrument back on its stand, he turned to her thoughtfully. "Your cousin has disappeared, Trina. It seems she's been gone a week now. There's been no word from her. Her husband"—he did not miss Petrina's quick flinch at the word—"has been out with a search party in the Glades near their home. That's why we haven't been able to raise him."

"A week?" She was bewildered. "That cable just arrived last night!"

Petrina dug the crumpled cable out of her raincoat pocket. "It was sent from Miami."

"Has she ever done anything like this before, Trina? That you know of?"

"I told you, I lived with Aunt Ellen for three years, after Dad died. She had adopted Linette when Linette was only five, so Linette was really like her own child, I guess. I don't know what might have happened to Linette before I arrived there. She never disappeared during any time I know of."

He looked at her curiously. "You never saw her until three years ago, then?"

"It's not so strange, David. My mother died when I was little and Dad never had much to do with her family, that I knew. He kept me with him or sent me off to boarding school."

She knew what he was thinking. She had known Tony Addison in Miami and she had brought him out to Cypress Glade to meet Aunt Ellen and Linette because he had asked her to marry him and she had accepted. She was playing the Top Hat in Miami Beach then. It was a week or two before Aunt Ellen had died. And three months later it was Linette, not Petrina, who was marrying Tony.

"I have to be going," David said. "Incidentally, did Morag remember to invite you to the party at her friend's flat tonight?"

Petrina shrugged.

And David grinned understandingly. "I know. But I'm bringing along a famous psychic, an old friend of mine, and I'd like to have you meet her." The twinkle left his eyes as he turned. "I'll pick you up at the theater and take you over. Who knows, I may be able to drag Julian along, too."

"I'll go."

He ran a finger gently along her cheek. "Good girl."

CHAPTER 3

The rain had gathered force by evening, slashing out in raw wet gusts that buffeted pedestrians and set them staggering as they tried to control umbrellas and make their ways along slick sidewalks. In the streets the streams of automobiles skidded and honked in mechanical ballets of avoidance that weren't always successful while their headlights weaved bleary patterns on the watery pavement.

But in spite of the storm outside, with the howl of wind punctuated frequently by the whoop of emergency claxons, Petrina was astonished to find that the theater was playing to almost a full house. Still, with a top-of-bill attraction like music-hall idol Sammy Stone, it would have taken a full gale to keep the crowd away. Everyone else on the bill benefited from the crowd's mood of happy anticipation.

Petrina felt it all through her own sketches, the Spanish with Pedro, the French with Apache Pierre, played against a projection of Montmartre and a gamy Left Bank bistro, the English with Peter against a filmed background of an ancient ruined castle. The audience clapped hard when she danced in splendid lonely elegance with Peter as room after empty room passed on the screen at the back and thin invisible music played softly to accompany the very old songs Petrina sang.

The English ball gown was stiff with brocade and heavy with brilliants that sent refracted light flashing from countless moving points. The brilliants were of fine quality, as satisfyingly perfect and varied in size and shade as real diamonds might have been. Their fire encircled her neckline and studded bodice and skirt so every movement of her body scattered radiant shafts.

Every cue had gone exactly right this evening. She and Katy had managed every costume change with smooth ease.

Now, if only she could have figured out some way to skip Morag's party after the show, everything would have been great. Though possibly, just possibly, David and his psychic friend, and Julian, if he could make it, might save that part of the evening from disaster.

She was thinking more of the rest of the evening than of the part of it just past as she reached out and punched her card in the time clock. Peter's carrying case was clasped as usual with her right hand and she had slung her shoulder bag securely left. Upon nearing the stage door she glanced expectantly over at the cubbyhole where old Timothy kept an eye on arrivals and departures. Tonight he eyed her with a twinkle, deliberately waiting her out.

Clearly David wasn't there. "No message from Mr. Nairac?" she asked finally, disappointed and trying unsuccessfully to conceal the fact.

He jerked his head toward the door. "A very personal message, Miss Gentry. In a manner of speaking, that is." He grinned, pleased with himself.

As the door sucked shut behind her, she looked up and down the deserted walkway, not quite sure what to expect. There was no sign of David Nairac here either. Crumpled programs swirled and stuck against the wet pavement as she continued on.

Slowly she walked up and down Argyll Street in front

of the theater, huddled into her raincoat, her shoes
quickly squishy with absorbed water.

Her throat tightened as she glanced up at the ghostly
bricks rising above her. Had her dad looked up like this
those years ago when he'd played here himself, with
Peter? The wind caught her coat and wrapped it around
her legs before sportively barreling on to the busy late
bustle of Piccadilly Circus.

Petrina's fingers tightened upon the handle of the case
that held the motionless form of Peter. A few stragglers
had set off on foot toward the lights of Piccadilly. Where
was David? He had said he'd pick her up.

There wasn't even a cab in sight. It was much too early
for the bevy of taxis to gather here at the curb for the
end of the second performance.

"Would you like a ride, luv?"

An unfamiliar sporty yellow convertible nipped in at
the curb and Petrina's eyes opened wide as David's grin
greeted her with affectionate amusement. "No, I didn't
lose my mind and buy it. Don't look at me like that." He
threw open the door on the passenger's side. "Jump in,
dear Trina, so I can make it back to the Prince before my
act comes on. I borrowed these wheels from Julian so he
could stay at the theater like a lazy slob and watch the
early acts. He hasn't had much chance to play lately, he
tells me."

"Sad stuff," she jeered, covering both her pleasure and
her relief at seeing him. "So there was his car right out in
front—much better than having to go all the way to the
parking area, wasn't it? Or was it the color that got to
you?"

"You found me out," he admitted. "Now get yourself in
this car or be prepared to walk!"

She had started to comply when they both froze.

The heavy roar of a truck approaching much too fast boomed down heavily traveled Oxford Street, a block away to the northwest. David's eyes narrowed as he grabbed the top of the door without pausing to reach for the handle and leaped out of the yellow auto.

A bulky nondescript truck rocked around the corner onto Argyle Street, screaming tires, and Petrina felt David's lean athletic body slam into her and his arms wrap around her as he carried her rolling along the wet sidewalk, away from the yellow sports car and flat against the shallow steps leading up to the front doors of the theater.

"Down," he ordered harshly. "Keep your head down, Trina!"

Petrina was too terrified to disobey. The sharp crack of gunfire echoed through theater arches and a second later an explosion sent a blast of air past them, followed by a rain of debris. David dragged her to her feet after the truck had passed by and ran with her up the shallow steps and into the shelter of the outer lobby, flattening her out of sight into a small alcove.

The truck came about and once more roared past, lighted by the now flaming torch of the yellow car. A few random shots ricocheted from stone and suddenly the lobby was surging with people.

"Are you all right, Trina?" David asked sharply. "Were you hurt?" His eyes were charcoal black against the gray-white of his face. "My God, Trina, were you injured?"

Petrina looked about in bewildered shock. "I'm all right, I think," she answered, then looked down at her empty hands. "Where is Peter?" she wailed. "Oh, David, I must have dropped Peter out there when the attack began!"

A policeman ran into the lobby from the street, in his grasp a crushed case from which Peter's head protruded, his ribald grin intact. Petrina rushed forward to take the ruins from him and clutch them close against her, tears welling into her eyes.

David took Petrina's arm and guided her back out to the street again and away from the almost burned-out car.

"Can I give you a lift, sir?" another policeman offered, opening the door of his vehicle. "They seem to have demolished your transportation. The young lady—is she all right or shall we get her to hospital?"

"No!" Petrina yelped, coming to life. "I won't go to a hospital! I'm perfectly all right! Don't you—"

"Thanks, Officer." David cut her short and handed her inside and settled beside her in the back seat. "I'll keep an eye on her and if she needs care later, I'll see that she gets it."

At the sound of David's voice, the policeman shot a glance of undisguised surprise up at the rear-vision mirror. David grinned ruefully. "We're headed for the Prince, Officer. You'll find my cousin Julian Farr there. We look a lot alike at a casual glance."

The policeman jerked his head in a nod of comprehension. "I understand, sir. Thank you, sir." The car pulled away from the curb and soon they were on Regent Street, heading toward Piccadilly Circus.

Petrina leaned back and closed her eyes, the crushed case containing Peter still held against her body. Tears ran unchecked down her cheeks and she turned her face toward the windows so David wouldn't see.

"Don't worry," David reassured her softly. "We'll have Peter repaired come morning. I'm sure the shop we were at this morning has a good repairman on call. Possibly Mr. Conolly himself. I'll go with you. Everything will be all right. You're a bit shocky now, but you will feel better soon."

"More than a bit shocky, David," she confessed, swallowing a hiccup and letting him settle her head back against his shoulder.

He began to tell her silly anecdotes about some of the people he had called from the audience during the mind-reading segment of his act and she relaxed to the sound of his voice, pleasant, authoritative. It had nothing to do with what he was telling her. It was the sure soothing quality of his voice itself that helped smooth away the panic.

"Sure you want to come in, now?" David's tone changed. "Do you feel up to Morag's party?" He really wanted an answer. "Do you want to change your mind and go back to your hotel?"

She slanted a look up at him as the car pulled out of traffic and cut in at the stage entrance at the Prince. "I'm sure."

As he helped her out, David turned toward the police-man. "Thank you, Officer. I'll tell Julian what happened immediately. You'd best wait right here, I think." The po-liceman nodded.

Petrina hurried along behind David, down a long corri-dor past dressing rooms and out finally into the warrens that led backstage. In the wings, tucked away so he could see the stage without interfering with stage business, sat a tall man bent-legged on a stool.

At first glance he bore a startling resemblance to David. He had the same lean rangy body as David's, the same thin face with hard-shadowed planes, the crest of dark hair brushed smooth. As he caught sight of David he unfolded in a lithe quick movement and came toward them and she saw even his eyes were like David's, keen and measuring, dark. But there were differences, too. He was older, perhaps by ten years, and there was a deadly tired droop to his shoulders and deep lines of strain bit deep on either side of his mouth.

David introduced him, then took him aside and rapidly

filled him in on what had happened. He told him a police car and driver were waiting for him outside.

"It looks to be a long night ahead for me," Julian surmised wryly after David had finished. "I doubt I will be able to join you for the party, my dears." He swore softly. "They were after me, I expect. They know my car and they must know I'm back from Belfast—and probably what I've been doing there. Their organization is good, really good.

"Right now they probably suspect I'm chasing down another of their damned IRA factories where they've been making their explosives. We've already found two bomb factories near Clapham Junction, but there are more. Always more terrorists and always more bombs. I just wish they were right about my locating the new place. Actually I haven't a clue as to where it might be."

He rubbed his hand across tired eyes and with a quick wave of his hand left.

Petrina went back to David's dressing room to wait for him. The room was quiet, large, a room given to a top-of-the-bill performer. He had turned off the lights around his mirror so that illumination came only from soft lamplight. With a sigh she sank down on a comfortable green patterned couch set against the wall and put Peter's battered case down beside her.

Muffled voices passed in the hallway, words indistinguishable, the safe normal sounds of working theater. Reaction set in suddenly and Petrina began to shake. For a few moments she could not control herself and it wasn't until she finally held her hands tightly clenched at her sides, fingernails biting painfully into palms, that the trembling lessened and finally stopped. She drew a deep harsh breath and leaned back against the soft support of the couch and closed her eyes.

It had been a close call, a very close call.

CHAPTER 4

The heavy rain had turned to drizzle and it was curiously comforting to Petrina to ride along beside David in his small black car again, the windshield wipers blipping back and forth companionably as the machine sped south, then east, toward the Thames. The familiar confines of the jaunty automobile seemed a secure barrier set against the encroachment of the terror they had faced earlier, holding it off, if only for a few hours.

Traffic thinned as David cut swiftly down several residential streets, then back to the garish color of King's Road, gaudy even in the rainy night.

"First we pick up my friend Catarina, who is a guest of people living near Cheyne Walk here in Chelsea. Very old and elegant and historic spot. Then we go on to Morag's flat, which she shares with three other girls who are playing at one of the theaters down here."

David slowed, searching for numbers along the rain-wet lines of stately Georgian houses standing tall and aloof behind their glistening ironwork fencings and galleries.

"Keep your eyes open for number 41," he ordered, rolling down his car window so he could see better. At the same instant his headlights caught the white gleam of the two numerals against a wrought-iron gateway and David pulled up at the curb.

Far below along the street, they could see the silvery ribbon of the Thames, spanned by the lovely spidery tracery of Albert Bridge, strung with lights, delicate against the night. Lamps glowed along the dark river wall, and here and there on the water lights outlined boats and barges and a cluster of houseboats moored at Whistler's Reach.

A light bloomed in the leaded-windowed hallway of number 41 and the heavy front door swung open. Outlined by the doorframe was a stout dumpy little figure enveloped in a shroudlike black gown, supporting herself with the aid of a utilitarian cane. She gestured impatiently as she exchanged last words with someone standing in the vestibule.

David ran up to the entry and clasped the sturdy figure in a big affectionate hug of greeting before he helped her carefully back to the car and into the back seat, out of the drizzle. The rain was far from over, but for the moment at least, it had slackened. David leaned around and made a brief introduction.

Nothing could have prepared Petrina for the impact of the bright black eyes that met hers with an intensity that seemed to reach down deep inside her for her most guarded secrets and to emerge with full knowledge of whatever it was Catarina had wanted to know.

"Catarina Régio," David had said.

The face was too much in shadow for Petrina to see it clearly but the eyes seemed clear and luminous with a life of their own. They were old eyes, eyes that had seen a great deal of sorrow as well as a large share of joy.

"*Sim.* You are the daughter of Robert Gentry who first gave life to the small crushed one who rides in the case beside me and who met with an accident tonight, *não?*"

Petrina stiffened and she caught the quick startled glance David sent toward the rear vision mirror. "You knew Trina's father?" David asked. "Why didn't you tell me?"

"First I wanted to meet her and be sure that this was indeed the daughter. How would it look I make pronouncement—and then you, the mentalist, you say, 'Aha! Catarina! You make mistake!'"

The brilliant eyes suddenly disappeared and Petrina realized the old woman had closed her eyes like curtains. For the time being, the conversation was over.

"Catarina is one of the world's great psychics," David briefed Petrina softly. "She is Portuguese. I first met her when we both were speakers at a psychic research conference in Mozambique, then another time when we were both in Rio de Janeiro at the same time, and we became friends. I need her help very badly tonight and I'm grateful that she came."

Petrina resisted the temptation to turn and observe the psychic. "I'm glad she came, too. It's always good to meet anyone who knew my father. I hope she will talk to me about him, later."

"Aren't you just a little curious about why I particularly wanted Catarina with us tonight?"

"You'll tell me." The certainty in her voice surprised Petrina as much as it did David. She hesitated uncertainly. "You will, won't you?"

"I can't tell you the whole story right now, Trina. But I'll be able to tell you some of it on the way home, I promise. It's better that you don't know more right now."

"I agree," Catarina Régio's voice accorded from the back seat. "If what you suspect to be true is actually true, then the less knowledge carried to this party, the better off a good many people will be."

David nodded. "The flat is in a multiple building back here, off Warder Lane. One of those miserable buildings first built and used by dock workers and their families and abandoned, and finally taken over by a pretty motley bunch."

He drove around the block slowly, scanning numbers, carefully eyeing the unpleasantly stripped ugliness of the row flats jammed along the narrow bumpy cobbled street.

"There it is," he announced triumphantly, at last. "That section closest to the intersection." He pulled the small black car skillfully into an inadequate space between an old truck and a disreputably disheveled Bentley.

Sounds of music and a mingling of laughter and voices came from the lower level of the corner flat and from behind the hazily curtained window moved the shadow figures of a varied collection of partygoers, some dancing, some moving decorously from one group toward another.

David herded his small party to the door, holding his umbrella carefully positioned as he punched the doorbell, once, twice. While they waited Petrina noted the sturdy cane Catarina carried and how expertly and needfully the psychic used it to make her way and balance herself.

"Do you think this Morag has the slightest idea of why you bring me?" Catarina asked urgently.

"No." David looked down at her with worry in his gaze.

"Good. This house has very bad psychic aura. It sounds like laughter and lighthearted pleasure but underneath it is hatred and anger—and something else. Something very much worse. We must watch out for your little one."

Petrina laughed nervously. "Oh, come now. I'm sure that Morag doesn't like me and that all her interest is in David—but you're making it sound—"

The door opened and a young woman drew them quickly in out of the drizzle. She was tall and slim, with the delicate pastel beauty sometimes found in young Englishwomen. Petrina sighed, examining the wide sea-blue eyes with their faint touch of lavender shadow. There was something about her very much like Linette, and she didn't want to think of Linette right then.

David asked for Morag and in just a few moments she appeared, bright and strident in scarlet chiffon to welcome them and take them about to be introduced to other guests. In the room was scrambled an odd assortment. Quite a few theatrical people were there, actors as well as music hall performers, several musicians. Some of the faces Petrina recognized from newspaper publicity, but there were many others with whom she was unfamiliar.

"Drink?" Morag led them to a buffet and got them started with drinks and food. "I'm so glad you could come." Her pale eyes were chilly on the two women, warm on David. "Your cousin couldn't make it?"

"He may still be along," David said. "I talked to him earlier this evening and he said he had some matters that needed attention first. A policeman's lot is a hard one."

Morag shrugged. "Whose isn't, luv?" Slowly she turned toward Catarina. For a long awkward interval she stared intently, leaning forward as though she were trying to absorb the older woman.

"You're an adept!" she cried out suddenly, her pale eyes narrowing. Her strong dancer's body gathered itself tensely as though she were about to spring in physical attack, or perhaps to defend herself—she seemed too distraught to know which.

Catarina watched her with regal distaste.

"*Por Deus do ceu!*" Catarina snapped. "Adept? At what? I do not understand!" Her black shoe-button eyes stared into Morag's ice-blue gaze and there was neither interest nor emotion expressed. Not only did she refuse to accept the accusation of esoteric witchcraft which Morag had flung, she refused even to comprehend what Morag implied. Petrina noticed a twitch of a smile quirk the corner of David's mouth.

Morag's gaze held for an instant, then became uncertain and finally fell.

"I am a psychic, with certain powers, of course," Catarina declared clearly. "No more than that. No less. Perhaps this is what you meant."

Petrina shivered as she stood beside the small self-possessed old woman. Something frightening was taking place in the warm festive room and she had no idea what it was. She took Catarina's arm and for an instant was shocked at the sensation of power that throbbed from it and into her own body. Controlling her first quick impulse toward withdrawal, she guided Catarina over to a nearby chair.

"Are you performing at any London hall?" Morag asked curiously, following. Clearly she did not quite believe what Catarina had told her and she was trying to find out more.

A flicker of amusement touched Catarina's eyes. "I am giving a few readings while I am in London, but only for clients who made their appointments long ago."

"I am disappointed."

"You wish a reading? I give you reading right now. But first I need a quiet place and I must have my two friends for battery. *Entendeu?* I am very weary this evening. The day has been busy and long and I am old."

"Just the four of us?" Morag asked, her pale eyes wide. "I'd like to include a few friends of my own."

Catarina thumped her cane against the floor. "I have no strength for games. If you want me to give you reading, we do it now and as I say. I don't care, myself. You are one who wants."

Attending the party had been a mistake, Petrina thought, just as she had anticipated it would be, only for a different reason. Whatever Catarina thought of the bad aura of the place, as a guest she had no business leading Morag on and then forcing this kind of argument.

David turned his head as though he had heard a message, soft enough to be hidden, but audible to him. "You'll help us out, won't you, Trina?" he asked. "If Morag wants to be read?"

And at that point Petrina realized that this never was a party at all for him, nor for Catarina either. They weren't bedeviling Morag for their own perverse entertainment. They were seriously challenging her in some way that Petrina could not fathom.

Without another word, Morag led the way to a small room off the living room, a kind of den, with book-lined walls, a small desk, and several uncomfortable chairs lined against the wall. Petrina selected one of them. Catarina settled herself in the big chair behind the desk with the aplomb of an old lady to whom comfort was an essential part of her requirements.

A deep flush colored Morag's cheeks momentarily, then swiftly faded. She took a seat beside Catarina, slivers of anger lightening her pale eyes. But she made no protest about the seating, nor about Catarina's manner. She wanted the reading to take place too, Petrina realized. No doubt she had from the second she recognized Catarina's name.

Catarina handed her cane to David for keeping and asked that the lights be turned off, all except for a very small decorative one thrust like a tiny flashlight into an outlet at knee height, apparently intended to be used as a night light. Catarina dropped her handkerchief over the fixture, further dimming the light. "Close your eyes, please. Concentrate."

David reached over and took Petrina's hand reassuringly as Morag leaned forward toward Catarina.

"Shall we begin?" Morag asked coldly.

A draft moved across the room and Petrina shivered. Catarina sat silent, her eyes closed, her body motionless. Morag, too, was silent and immobile.

"I see water, part of a sea and beyond it hills and cliffs and mist and green covering the land. Ireland." Catarina's voice, heavily accented, was difficult to hear. "I see mountains and woodland and people dancing in the moonlight."

The scene Catarina was describing began to play behind Petrina's eyes like the movie backgrounds she used in her sketches with Peter. She felt a wind heavy with the fragrance of mountain evergreen sweep across her face and in a grove she saw a circle of bodies, unclothed and shadowy, weaving in a circle before a tall burly creature seated on a crude chair that seemed to serve as a throne.

"No!" Morag protested, lunging forward. "No!" She seemed tied invisibly to her chair in spite of her efforts to arise.

As though an eraser had removed the scene, the trees and the mountain and the bodies were gone. Out of the shapeless black came only soft amorphous clouds.

"Of what interest could be the initiation rites of one young girl into a coven of witches?" Catarina's mocking voice pierced the quiet. "And did they lead you to think you could do *anything* with your training?"

The soft clouds began to form into gray walls and streets, the drab buildings and streets of a northern city, policed by army vehicles, its air rent by explosives and the screams of terrified children and mourning women and the dying.

Petrina cried out in fear. The explosion and the fire were out of the same piece of terror that David and she had witnessed. And they emanated from the same source.

"Belfast," David said softly.

The scene changed again and Petrina saw the creamy

stone of the Berwyck rising against a lowering sky. Again she felt the concussion of the explosion and the fear and her own voice crying out as David protected her body with his own.

This terror was connected with the other.

Here in this room, behind the scenes, she could sense a private battle taking place, two women struggling to gain access and control of the secrets being enacted against the screens of their minds. She felt David's strength calling on her own and passing it on to the old woman sitting in the big chair behind the desk.

The Berwyck remained against the screen of Petrina's mind, held there as though one of the women would not or could not let it go. This was not part of the previous scene, Petrina thought suddenly. This scene was for the future, a *planned* scene, not one which had already taken place.

People began to fill the broad pavement and the sky now behind the Berwyck was bright with the sunshine of afternoon. The audience was filling the theater for an afternoon matinee. Horror rose through Petrina's body, wrenching every cell, thickening the warmth of her blood with a freezing chill.

A faceless man walked in with the audience, a brightly decorated clothing-store box under his arm, an innocuous box, not to be suspected. In the box was death—not for the sunny afternoon but for the dark shadowy night. He would set his explosive charges during the matinee. Someone else would detonate them at the crowded evening performance.

Petrina gasped, her fingers closing hard on David's arm.

The door to the small dark den opened abruptly and light from the living room flooded violently in upon them. Petrina squeezed her eyes tight against the painful invasion and Morag gasped a horrified choking cry before she slumped out of her chair and slid to the floor. David moved slowly, stiffly, coming to his feet.

"What's going on here?" an intruding male growled hoarsely. Beside him stood the woman who had opened the door.

"Morag . . ." the woman rushed into the room and leaned down over the limp body on the floor. "She promised to call us—"

"She will be all right," Catarina said calmly, pushing them back with sheer will power and the astonishing dignity of her manner. She took her cane from David and stood up slowly, bracing herself against the desk top with her other hand. "These games we play can sometimes be dangerous." She marched with effort over to the body on the floor. "She will remember nothing of this when she regains consciousness," Catarina said. "She will remember nothing."

"Come." David extended his arm and Catarina took it gratefully. "You all right, Trina?" he asked. "They will take care of Morag. Don't worry. She really will be all right soon. It's time for us to leave."

Not a trace of festive atmosphere remained as they walked to the front door past a phalanx of hostile faces making no attempt at all to conceal their anger. Something more than simple anger made the air heavy and charged its particles. David opened the front door and helped Catarina through it, held out his hand to Petrina.

"What about Julian?" Petrina asked. "He mustn't walk into that place."

"He won't," David assured. "He would have been there by now if he had been able to make it."

CHAPTER 5

The jangle of the telephone bell pierced Petrina's early morning nightmare and shocked her to sudden consciousness. Heart pounding as she blinked away the remembered sight and sound of bombs and flame, she reached out swiftly, almost knocking the instrument to the floor.

"How are you doing?" David's voice inquired cheerfully from the telephone. "Feeling better?"

"Better?"

She thought about the silent ride from Morag's house to the elegant town house where a light through leaded windows awaited the return of Catarina Régio to Cheyne Walk. And about the ride back to the hotel with David escorting her into the lobby, to find Julian Farr waiting for them, his face gray with fatigue.

"Are you there?" David prodded anxiously. "Petrina!"

"Oh, I'm here, all right," she assured him. "I surely am. David, I'm starving."

She could hear him laugh, a nice gusty relieved male sound. When she'd watched him leave with Julian last night she had wondered if either David or Julian would survive to laugh again. "David, where are you?"

"Down in the lobby, pet. Get dressed and come down and I'll buy you breakfast and regale you with fascinating facts."

A quick shower splashed away most of the cobwebs

left from sleep. She pulled on a yellow jersey dress that made her look a lot perkier than she felt. Over on the dressing table lay the case and on it broken Peter. On the floor at the end of the bed lay the Colonel. There was no use fussing with either of them yet. Breakfast was the immediate project. After breakfast she could face almost anything.

The lift was only a short distance down the corridor. She got on and finished combing out the damp ends of her hair as she rode slowly down the five floors to the lobby. Just as she had fluffed the last soft strand, the elevator jolted to a halt with a grind of labored gears.

David was leaning against the dark paneled wall of the lobby near the elevator, a copy of the morning *Express* in his hand, his dark eyes intent on the story he was reading. When he caught sight of her he folded the newspaper and tucked it under his arm.

There were a few guests already occupying some of the chairs scattered about the lobby. At his post behind the registration counter, the desk clerk looked up with discreet curiosity. David swept Petrina along into the coffee shop off to the left.

With a tired smile David seated her and opened the menu which a brisk soap-scented waitress deposited in front of him. "Coffee," he ordered. "Immediately. Hot. Lots of it." While Petrina read her own menu he continued, "Muffins with marmalade. Scrambled eggs, grilled tomatoes and mushrooms. And what, ham? Kippers? Orange juice?" He halted and fixed Petrina with an inquiring stare. "All of that?" he demanded incredulously, before she could answer. "Very well, then!"

The waitress giggled and hurried off.

"Really bad?" Petrina asked.

David sighed and dropped his jaunty attitude. "Really bad, Trina. I told Julian what happened at Morag's party.

They have been keeping an eye on her activities, incidentally. The combination of her politics and her friends and her mobility as a professional dancer all have made her very interesting to the Anti-Terrorist Squad."

The waitress slipped cups of steaming coffee in front of them and placed a napkined basket of hot muffins on the table with a pot of English marmalade and a plate of butter pats.

"Did you get any sleep at all last night?" Petrina asked, watching as David sipped his coffee.

"None. But at least I have no performances today." He sighed and ran his hand through his dark hair. "While we were busy at the party, Julian was pressed into service on a long planned raid on two IRA bomb factories, one in Brigston and the other in Clapham Junction. Both were typical, he told me, of the kind of place most of the terrorists favor, a couple of 'short lets'—furnished flats—in Irish neighborhoods. The squad made quite a haul, of explosives and men both. And Julian thinks they found the truck used in the attack on us. No question about it now, Julian was supposed to be the target when the attack was made at the theater. He must have been followed for quite a while. They didn't realize that it was I and not Julian who left the Prince in his car."

Petrina crumbled a muffin between fingers that suddenly trembled. "Last night, while you and Catarina were—when Catarina was doing the reading—" She stopped, not knowing how to put into words the scene that had flashed across her mind, of demolition at the theater, and the feeling that it was planned for the future, not something from the past. She wanted it to have been her imagination, a result of the whole overwrought encounter.

His dark eyes studied her reflectively. "If you are asking whether Catarina might have been wrong in what she read last night, the answer is yes. A psychic is not dealing with a concrete physical reality but with a personal perception of it. She could have misinterpreted what she received. But if you are asking whether I think she was wrong, the answer is no."

"Thank you." But she wasn't quite satisfied and he knew it.

"Julian thinks the terrorists plan another go at the theater," he said. "Catarina and Julian are friends of long standing, incidentally. He trusts her intuition about such a matter, whatever psychic factor might or might not be involved in her suggesting that another attack might take place."

"Does he have any idea how or when they might act?"

"None."

"Why does he think they'd choose the Berwyck rather than some other theater?" she asked, chilled as she realized that the threat had become a very personal one now.

"Lots of good reasons. It seats some twenty-four hundred people. It's the second largest house in London and the most famous variety house in the world. Besides that, the terrorists have been striking at some of the stores in Oxford Street and they seem to prefer to work the vein out, group their efforts. The Berwyck is in the vicinity of their other activity."

The difficulty at yesterday's matinee and Morag's appearing to know the man who substituted at the control panel assumed new significance to Petrina and she told David about it. He listened with intent interest.

"I'll pass that on to Julian before we take Peter out to have him repaired."

"Oh, that's what we're going to do?"

He looked down into her mocking hazel eyes with a

wry grin. "Just be glad I'm still in motion," he admonished. "You really can't expect gallantry too, can you?"

Before they had finished their meal, she remembered something else. "Morag said that she told you about the doll shop and the Colonel," she said.

"She did tell me about it." David sipped his coffee. "But so did Julian and several other people. That doll shop is very well known. Conolly's work is reliable and he has always gotten good help." The lines of weariness in David's face deepened. "It's just too bad that he happens to be so expert in the other less advertised types of trade he engages in.

"British intelligence knows he's involved with the IRA. They know many of the people who go in and out of his shop aren't there to buy dolls or have them repaired. But he's more useful left alone and watched than harried. His premises are not used to make or hold explosives."

"Sure?" She was doubtful.

He nodded. "Positive. But that could change in a hurry. Are you finished?"

"Thank you, David—yes."

He settled his check and they exchanged the brightness of the coffee shop for the dimness of the lobby. While David called Julian on a public telephone, Petrina went up to her room to pick up Peter and his case. David had finished his conversation when she returned. His newspaper was still under his arm.

"Was there a story about the explosion?" she asked.

"No." They walked across the lobby and out into the bright sun of the day. "No one was killed so I suppose it wasn't considered news." He guided her to his car parked down the block. "There was another jewel robbery in Ennismore Gardens Mews, though, and the haul was enough to finance quite a few bombs, if Julian's theory is right. He thinks the rash of jewel thefts in some of the posh areas around here helps to finance terrorist activities. That some of the girl friends of the men work as domestics and finger the jewelry."

Despite the warm radiance of the morning, in such contrast to the day before, Petrina felt cold. She tried to concentrate on profuse displays of spring blossoms, in window boxes, spilling over from countless hanging baskets, crowding against the trim iron railings that bounded tiny beautifully tended dooryard gardens. Flamboyant fuchsias in improbable glowing shades, yellow jonquils and freesias. Tulips raising deep cups of flame and gold and infinite variations in between, hyacinths in purples, lavenders, whites, pinks, dispensing fragrance on the air even from a distance.

But the color and fragrance diminished, then disappeared after they left the well-kept fine residential neighborhoods and began to follow the shabby streets that led them closer to the doll shop. Petrina's tension increased with every block.

"Did you know the city has a competition for best window boxes?" David asked gently, to distract her.

She smiled wanly. "I keep thinking of what could happen if they planted a bomb in the theater—or even threw one in the lobby, for that matter. With the audiences we're drawing, it would be a calamity."

He drew a deep breath and didn't look toward her at all.

"There's nothing I can say about that to make you feel better, Trina. I was here a few years ago when they bombed the Old Bailey, the criminal court—there were a lot of casualties. Bombs exploded in two busy train stations not much later and there were deaths and injuries.

A bomb exploded in Harrod's department store, where Queen Elizabeth shops sometimes. I'm just mentioning things that happened when I have been here in London."

"There's not much to do and nowhere to go, is there?" she said slowly.

"There are a few things to do. There are a lot of men like Julian working to halt the terrorists. Life doesn't stop just because fanatics kill innocent people—life can't be allowed to stop because of fear."

"Thank you, David."

He shook his head ruefully. "Still, I wish you weren't here and playing this particular theater at this particular time. I wish—"

"Don't say it. If Peter can be repaired enough to be operative, I'm not going to miss a performance. Besides, there is no way of knowing when they plan their strike, nor even for sure that they *have* planned it. As you said, life can't stop because of them."

She was perversely pleased to see that he was frowning, worried.

For a few blocks he drove in silence. "It was Julian who suggested we go back to this shop," he said finally. "There are other shops, of course. If you'd rather we didn't—"

"I thought that might have entered into it. He's right. We might notice something that could help him."

"Just so you know."

He slowed down as they passed a row of drab council houses that gave on older run-down flats and shops. Very seriously he asked, "Can you conduct yourself with detachment, at least enough so we don't precipitate something we can't handle?"

She hadn't thought of the actual encounter. "Yes." She would have to think of it as a sketch, a dialogue between Mr. Conolly and herself.

"Pengable Street." David turned the corner and pulled in to the curb.

The shabby doll shop looked different, somehow, in the pitiless revelation of a sunny day. The stone of the entry stoop was gray, with hollows worn by the feet of countless customers over generations long gone. The rotting wood that framed the entrance door showed traces of paint that had flaked so many years ago that only thin traces of color remained along the grain of the wood. The sun reflected off the dirty windows without reaching inside to illuminate them.

David swung the door open for her and followed her, carrying the case with Peter inside.

"Good morning," Mr. Conolly said warily, from his station behind the display counter. "Mr. Nairac. Miss Gentry—and how did you like the Colonel?" He didn't really smile. His mouth widened to bare his teeth and his skin creased horizontally along his bony face.

"Very well indeed." Petrina watched as David placed Peter's case on the counter and drew out the doll. "I was involved in an automobile accident last night in front of the theater and Peter was damaged. Fortunately his head wasn't hurt, but his controls seem a bit sprung. Could you go over him and fix what needs it so he will be in service for the matinee this afternoon?"

There was no one else in the shop, no sound of voices from the back area.

Mr. Conolly took the damaged doll up in his thin hands and went over the outside. Then he slipped a hand up inside and his eyes narrowed as he moved Peter's arms, hands. He tried the eyes, mouth, head. "It looks worse than it is," he pronounced with the authority and dignity of a surgeon. "I can have it ready for you to pick up at noon. Actually most of the damage seems to have been done the case. Would you like to buy a new one?"

Discard the case the great Robert Gentry had passed on down to his daughter with his beloved puppet?

"I'll buy a new one but I want the old one repaired. No hurry on it. I can use the new one later on to carry his costumes in, whatever. But while we're here, I'd like to see the two Pedlar dolls again." She looked down into the fingerprint-smeared glass of the case. "They aren't here! Mr. Conolly, we told you we'd be back for the one I wanted! You haven't sold it, have you?"

"I put it aside for you. But I wanted to do a little tightening of the wares in the basket. I noticed some of the miniatures have come loose. Supposing I go ahead with the task and have both your ventriloquist's doll and the Pedlar ready for you when you return?"

The almost fleshless skin of his face tightened as he waited for her answer. His eyes were blank and opaque, staring from shuttered lids.

"All right."

As though her agreement had offered a solution to an urgent problem with which he was faced, he smiled again, this time with nervous relief. "I'll see you at noon, then, Miss Gentry!" He was almost quivering with his obvious eagerness to get at his tasks.

"You're sure you know which of the Pedlars I wanted?" Petrina persisted. "It was the one on the left. It was prettier and I liked its expression better."

Mr. Conolly's face went as immobile as a skull stretched with gray parchment. "I know which one you want," he said, nodding. "Be assured of that."

Petrina felt David's hand, warm and reassuring, on her arm.

"Thank you," she told Mr. Conolly uncertainly. "I'll be back."

His mouth stretched back across his teeth. "Yes. Of course you will."

CHAPTER 6

"You have three messages here, Miss Gentry."

Petrina had been aware of the registration clerk's appreciative glance from the moment she marched through the big doors that the uniformed doorman held wide for her.

She smiled at him with the sunny shining look that her father once told her would be all the dowry she need ever bring to her husband to make him happy.

But that thought led too fast to another. Robert Gentry had been very wrong about how a smile might stack up against a dowry, she thought astringently. He had never known Tony Addison. Tony had been satisfied to be engaged to Petrina's smile, but when it came time to marry, it was Linette's newly inherited estate he found a lot more attractive.

The smile left her face. "Thank you, Mr. Billingsley."

The desk clerk's expression became flatly businesslike. "There is this message from the overseas operator, to call the number I have written down here, in Florida. We received the call shortly after you and Mr. Nairac left this morning. That was about nine-fifteen, the precise time is on the memo. They asked that you return the call as soon as you returned." His eyes brightened with interest as he realized fully what he had said. "Five-hour difference— that would make it five in the morning there, wouldn't it? A bit early, unless it's an emergency. Well, that was the message. The other two calls were local."

She tucked the message memos in her handbag and started away.

"Mum, we heard what happened last night at the theater and we feel badly about it, all of us. It's a terrible thing."

She focused every lumen of her best smile full on him in thank you. "My father played the halls and camps during the Blitz and he always felt he was sharing the nation's trouble. It's much the same these days, isn't it?"

"You could say that." His shoulders squared. "Yes, I suppose you could say that, indeed."

The lift was waiting. She stepped in, and after it had started toward her floor, she drew out the memos and began to read them. Somehow she had expected the name on the record of the Florida call to be that of Sam Brock, the lawyer. She saw "Tony Addison" instead, with shock. Her knees went weak and she tensed in a panic as paralyzing as though Tony himself would be waiting in person when the lift reached her floor and the door jolted open.

He might have reached her this morning, *would* have if David had not come by and taken her with him.

So much for all the fine new directions of life, she thought, shaken.

A year ago, fresh from the brutal experience of having been dropped callously, all she had been able to handle was personal survival. And she had managed that only by walling away all of the memories and emotions associated with Tony.

The wall wasn't very thick, she thought, when just the unexpected sight of his name could do this to her. Or was it the knowledge that quite easily she could pick up the telephone and this time he would be on the other end of the line, waiting to hear from her? How many times had she left messages for Tony to call—and waited—and waited—in those dreadful days before he finally told her that their engagement was over?

She threw back her head and began to laugh a little wildly, stopped as she saw a chambermaid stare at her disapprovingly over the top of a trolley full of cleaning supplies. The maid remained puttering with her supplies, watching suspiciously, until Petrina finally found her key in the clutter of purse and let herself in.

Once in the privacy of her room, Petrina opened the other two messages. One was from the theater. The other was from Catarina Régio.

Tony's message she put aside. When she put in her call to Cypress Glade, and now she knew she would have to do it herself, the call would be to Sam Brock and it wouldn't be until afternoon, perhaps two o'clock or so, so she would catch Mr. Brock when he first arrived at his office. She didn't want to hear the sound of Tony's voice, cajolingly affectionate, manipulative, covering the truth of whatever happened to him with a false veneer of words.

When the switchboard answered at the hotel, she gave the theater telephone number.

In a few minutes she was connected with Nora Talson, the very efficient secretary who reigned over the outer office of the theater's manager, Mr. Boyton.

"Terribly sorry to learn of your unfortunate encounter last night," Nora said brightly. "Mr. Boyton tried to get you earlier to tell you so and to tell you that we have arranged a substitute for your turns today, both matinee and evening. That should give you time to have poor Peter and yourself restored a bit."

"Thank you." Petrina explained about the arrangements to have Peter repaired, but the secretary brushed aside any talk of trying to give a performance.

"Mr. Boyton is a great believer in the stiff upper lip,"

she said pleasantly. "But really, pet, it doesn't have to be quite that stiff, you know. Mr. Boyton says we really do owe you one, anyhow. You must have done him quite a favor, to deserve an unscheduled day off."

Petrina was puzzled as she returned the telephone to its stand. That was a curious way to phrase it. Mr. Boyton owed her a favor? For being part of the reason for the incident in front of his theater? Perhaps the secretary had misunderstood.

She gave the switchboard girl Catarina Régio's telephone number and waited patiently. At last she hung up. The Portuguese psychic was not at the number she had left.

It was almost ten-thirty. She kicked off her shoes and removed the jersey dress, hanging it across a nearby chair. David had gone back to his hotel to get some reviving rest in before he picked her up to return to the doll shop. That would be a good idea for her, too. She set her alarm clock for eleven in case she fell asleep, and drew her blinds against the bright sunlight. With a sigh she settled herself upon the inviting flatness of her bed and closed her eyes.

For a few moments she dozed in the dim quiet with the traffic noises down on the street muffled by closed windows and blinds and the soft hum of the air conditioner. She let her bones go soft and her mind wander as she tried one of the relaxing techniques David had taught her. It didn't work.

Instead, pictures began to form against her eyelids, disturbing scenes, lonely scenes. Uncountable miles of tall saw-toothed grass with shimmering water gleaming beneath it and tall tufts of hammocks scattered at long intervals. There were no faces, no people. She saw the house at Cypress Glade, very large, threateningly Victorian, perched in the middle of its humped hammock. And she saw the wonderful wild twisted trees of Big Cypress, saw the thrusting lungs of trees that breathed in their own fashion in a strange primeval swamp world.

She felt it call, drawing her like a thin voice that lay endlessly on the humid air.

With a start she came to consciousness, her heart pounding, fear choking her. For a few moments she lay panting, having to orient herself to the present, to the safety of her hotel room here in the center of London, to the busy hum of traffic outside and the bustle of thousands of people going about their business in this great city.

It was almost eleven o'clock, she saw by her watch.

As she regained control of herself, she let her eyelids close slowly, experimentally, shutting out her hotel room again. She waited with the sharp sour taste of fear in her throat for the pictures to resume, this time ready to erase them with the quick action of wakefulness.

When the lonely stretches of swamp did not resume their substance, she tried deliberately to bring them back, by remembering the great echoing vastness of the old house itself, the massive carved furniture, the crowded bookcases in the musty study, the galleried bedrooms on the second floor with their wide views of the spreading acres beneath.

The remembered scenes were lifeless, like photographs, even when they involved Linette and Aunt Ellen. They had nothing of the threatening living quality of the pictures to which she had awakened.

Suddenly she felt a gentle warmth reach out and envelop her and she thought of David. She was thinking of his strength, his kindness, and beyond that something else, something dark, a mixture of joy and promise when she slipped off again into a doze, this time dreamless and serene, as though somewhere a guard had been posted to ensure her peace.

CHAPTER 7

David was prompt, framed in the big doors of the lobby at exactly eleven-thirty. His tall lean frame moved with lithe efficiency and he appeared as alert and rested as though he'd enjoyed a fine full night's sleep. His eyes swept the ranged chairs and divans, examining each face, gentled as he found her tucked against a winged green velvet chaise longue like a yellow jonquil on moss.

"Catarina invited us for lunch," he told her, on the way to his car. "I took the liberty of accepting for both of us."

"Good. I'm glad." Reluctant to allow Tony to intrude on the morning, even by reference to him, she didn't tell David about Tony's telephone message until they had almost reached the doll shop.

"Did you return his call?" David asked mildly, but his dark eyes were hooded and he kept them fixed on the busy street.

"No." She was interested in his reaction. "I decided to wait and place a call to Mr. Brock instead. After we'd finished at the doll shop. I didn't want to talk to Tony. About anything."

"You didn't?" A faint smile curved David's lips for an instant. Then he frowned. "Trina, I wish we could know what is actually going on over there. We're having to assume too much. For instance, we can assume right now that it is unlikely that Tony is calling to tell you that Linette has been found. We can assume that because the didn't get in touch with you in the first place when she disappeared, so why would he if she reappeared? He could have reached you, you know. Linette thought of making contact with Ken Evens. He could, too. Agents aren't that hard to locate when you're trying to find a performer. He must have gotten your number from Mr. Brock after I talked to Brock last night. That means the two of them do a fair amount of note swapping."

"Are you using logic or extrasensory perception to arrive at that?"

The corner of his mouth quirked. "Logic."

"That's reassuring." She slanted a measuring glance up at him.

The parking areas around the doll shop were so congested they didn't find a spot for themselves until toward the end of the next block. But that gave them a chance to dawdle and enjoy the warmth of noonday, to watch passing faces and to listen to the cadence of voices, liquid Irish leavened with solid British basic. Petrina filed away a few overheard earthy exchanges in her memory, then turned her attention to David again.

"Fine mentalist you are," she baited him. "You shouldn't have to surmise. You should be able to *know* where Linette is and what she's up to."

"I just know the numbers on watches and the amount and serial numbers of money some stranger has in his wallet," David grinned amiably. "And what someone is thinking about. Dumb things like that. But I'm poor at useful things, like knowing where Linette might be. She would have to send me a telepathic message for that and I hardly think she's likely to do so."

She flushed. "You can't really read people's minds, can you? It's illusion, isn't it? And showmanship and a bit of luck?"

"Something like that." His saturnine face was alight with teasing amusement. "It has to be, doesn't it? Otherwise, who on earth could stand to be around me? Wouldn't do at all!"

She eyed him suspiciously and was relieved as he threw back his head and laughed with delight at having flustered her.

When they were crossing the street, Petrina was aware of a burly workman who paced them to the left, listening to their conversation with unusual interest. The man dropped back a step or two as they reached the curb and he continued on down the block when they turned into the doll shop entrance.

"You really can't, can you?" Petrina asked again.

"You do sound disappointed," David observed. "However, supposing someday I hypnotize you? I can really do a good job on that. I could even do it when you were wide awake and alert—possibly you wouldn't even know I was doing it. How would that be?"

Horrified, she turned on him to see if he had meant it and he was quickly apologetic.

"I'm sorry, Trina. Sometimes I can't resist teasing you, but I'm truly sorry that I made you uncomfortable. You asked if I can read minds and that's hard to answer simply. You know that a mentalist uses trained telepathic ability, if he doesn't rely on plants in the audience—and if he's any good. I have some telepathic ability—everybody has—and I've trained it. But I don't walk around like a radar with its dishes revolving, psychically speaking. As a matter of fact, it takes a lot of concentration and energy to do the show and I don't think anyone could be *on* all of the time, onstage and off, both. I know I couldn't."

She shot a coolly evaluating look up at him without answering.

"Look at it this way," he coaxed. "Most of the things people think about aren't very exciting. Grocery lists. Appointments with the doctor. Fights and arguments. Little secrets that nobody on earth besides themselves really cares about. The first discipline I had to learn was how to turn *off* the barrage of unsolicited information." His dark eyes were troubled.

"All right," Petrina conceded. "I understand what you're saying." She tried to explain herself in return. "It isn't that I have so blasted many secrets or that they're so fascinating or dark, but they're *mine*. I don't like the idea of someone, even you, walking uninvited into my mind."

"I know." He opened the door for her. "Even if I could, I would never intrude on your privacy, Trina."

Mr. Conolly saw them and brought out Peter's repaired case immediately. He stood by, composed and confident of his work. He had managed a remarkable job of emergency construction, with sections of the old case retained wherever possible, and new boards substituted where damage had been too extensive.

"I'd like to have been able to keep it a bit longer so I could stain the new wood and varnish it and make it look more presentable. This does the job, but it does look rough."

Petrina opened it and removed Peter so she could examine him and test his mechanics. Mr. Conolly had done a fine job there, too. Peter felt as good as ever; in fact his head suspension had been improved. She moved her hand carefully over the strong rubber cord that ran from one side of Peter's body to the other, holding his head at the right tension through the head shaft's screw eye down inside the doll's shelf.

"You've changed this," she said. "I like it much better— I can use more natural movements." She illustrated for them, the usual side to side, forward, backward, then an over-the-shoulder, a stretch. "I'll take him along now," she decided. "The appearance of his case doesn't matter all that much, as long as I can carry Peter and some of his things safely in it. But I don't like to have Peter out of my reach if I can help it."

Mr. Conolly nodded his skull-like head and his lips pulled back in his strained smile. "All right, then, Miss Gentry. I have your bill ready for you. And I have made out the statement you will need to bring the Pedlar doll into the States as an antique. You won't have to pay duty that way. I put the doll in a padded box so it will be able to travel safely whatever its journey. Here is the bill, all totaled for you."

She wrote out a check for him on the City bank account to which her salary was deposited. The excellent work on Peter and his case came to a charge of less than one hundred dollars, and the price of the Pedlar doll was slightly under three hundred, bringing the total to much less than she had expected, even at the current exchange rate.

"You did a splendid job, Mr. Conolly, and I am most appreciative."

His expression remained a disconcertingly fixed smile. "You're welcome, Miss Gentry. Yes. Indeed." His flat uninflected speech gave the ordinary rejoinder a strangely threatening flavor.

David carried Peter off in the case and left the Pedlar doll to Petrina.

The breezy sun-warmed air outside felt good after the musty dim closeness of the shop. Shivering in reaction, Petrina tucked the rectangular awkwardness of the Pedlar's wrapped package under her arm.

"I'm glad we're finished with Mr. Conolly," she told David heartfeltly. The shop seemed to stare out at the street inimically through the opaque eyes of is dirty windows. "I don't like that place. I don't like that man."

"Pax," David smiled. "I don't like him either but he's behind us. We've got the job done."

With Peter and the Pedlar doll stowed snugly in the

trunk, David took a meandering course toward Catarina's apartment. He followed the Thames past the new London Bridge, built to replace the old one, which had been sold to an Arizona consortium and moved to America stone by stone. The expensive new bridge which had taken its place had one critical flaw, however. While it was twice as wide as the old, the new bridge had been built with approaches too narrow to take the projected traffic.

Gradually Petrina's tension began to abate as she listened to David's running commentaries. That was what he intended, of course. His dark eyes touched her briefly.

As they crossed back over the Thames on Lambeth Bridge, one of the older bridges, the magnificent buildings of the houses of Parliament slid by. David glanced at his watch. "We'd best head for Chelsea. Someday I'm going to come back to London as a tourist and do nothing else for months but wander and examine and study."

He set course along Grosvenor Road and turned north when they reached Chelsea Bridge Road. His eyes were hidden behind his dark glasses and he had fallen into a preoccupied silence.

Swinging the little black car around the corner at Cheyne Walk, he pulled it up short before number 41. The house stood pristine and elegant with the early afternoon sun picking out immaculate blooms behind its trim iron railing. David pulled off his sunglasses but his dark eyes were no more readable when she could see them than they were when she couldn't.

"Trina—"

Before he could say more, the heavy front door swung wide framing Catarina in a shapeless black dress, braced against her cane.

"*Boa tarde, queridos!*" she called. "You are late! Please to bring along the dolls that I may see them!"

David looked up at her, surprised. "The dolls?" He

nodded with sudden comprehension. "Psychometry. *Bem.
Obrigado,* Catarina!"

Catarina waited for them at the top of the short flight
of steps. "My hostess could not be here to meet you but
she tells me to make you welcome and she hopes you will
enjoy your lunch!"

Small glasses of excellent madeira were served them in
a very formal drawing room before they continued on to
a plant-banked solarium where lunch was served. Petrina
watched the interplay between David and the elderly
psychic with interest. On the surface they enjoyed the
airy omelets before them, and the crisp water-cress and
sliced tomato salad. But beneath the surface amenities
something entirely different was taking place.

"You left the dolls in the drawing room, *sim?*"

David inclined his head. "Yes."

The maid removed their plates and brought in sugar-
rimed crystal bowls filled with perfect bright strawberries
swimming in country cream.

Catarina signaled the maid to offer an ornate platter
studded with tiny succulent cakes. "The rum sponge is
good, and the *queljadinhas de amêndoas.* These flans."
She took nothing for herself.

"A Portuguese refuses a sweet?" David shook his head
in mocking dismay. "You really do have your mind on the
project ahead, don't you?" He finished his coffee and
pushed the cup away.

"These dolls have been handled at the shop?" Catarina
asked reflectively. "Intimately? Long enough to have become useful?"

A frisson rippled along Petrina's skin.

David nodded.

"May I see these dolls now?" Catarina moved heavily
to her feet. She asked David a question in rapid Portuguese and without understanding what was said, Petrina
knew the question was asked about her.

"*Não*," David answered crisply. "It's all right. Let's get on with it, Catarina."

They returned to the drawing room and David opened the case containing the ventriloquist's doll, drew Peter out, placed him in Catarina's hands.

"This is a very old doll." Catarina held Peter gently for a few moments and put him aside. "It holds a confusion of images but the strongest are of love and happiness in working with this fellow." She put the doll down on the sofa. "He tells us nothing. The contact with him at the shop was merely that of mechanical repair."

Petrina opened the packaging around the Pedlar doll and drew out the colorful figure. "This one is old, too," she said. "Much older than Peter."

For the first time she really examined the Pedlar. It was a far more unusual doll than she had thought in the first place, beautifully fashioned with a stuffed body made of hand-sewn leather, with wooden limbs and an exquisite papier-mâché face. The Pedlar was a woman with a red woven cape, red bonnet, white apron. Upon her tray were secured several miniature books, a red velvet cap with a dull silver ornament, a pewter goblet, a pierced silver fan—in all a wide assortment of miniatures scaled to the doll's height of approximately eleven inches.

"This doll doesn't have a maker's name or date on its tray, but it is similar to the C. and H. White dolls made in the New Forest," Petrina said softly. "About eighteen-twenty. I saw a genuine one in the London Museum." She held the doll carefully, her eyes going from the fascinating tray to the white face with its smug— Her breath caught. "David, this is the wrong doll! This isn't the one I picked out yesterday, it's the one that was in the case next to it!"

Catarina held out her hands and Petrina gave her the doll. Catarina leaned over it, her eyes closed, and the force of her concentration kept Petrina and David silent, watching her. Suddenly those astonishing deep-set black eyes opened wide.

"*Meu Deus do ceu*," Catarina breathed. "This doll has indeed been the object of terrible thoughts. Hatred and greed. Intrigue. Rivalry. Death." Her face was suddenly drained and old. "This doll must go back to the man who sent it along with you. Immediately."

David bent and kissed her cheek. "*Obrigado*. We will take it back at once, before we return to Trina's hotel. I will let you know later how it went. You must rest now."

"I thank you, too, Senhora Régio." Petrina bundled the wrappings hurriedly around the doll while David got Peter and his gear together. Petrina's heart pounded a hard pulse in her throat as she dashed outside, hastening along toward a confrontation so frightening to think of that only David's presence beside her made the trip possible.

After David had hurled the small black car out into traffic and across town, she began to regain some of her composure.

"David, what on earth could possibly be so terrible about a doll worth only a few hundred dollars? I do want to return it and get the doll I chose, but we don't have to be in such a frantic rush, do we? Might not your friend have overreacted to what will no doubt turn out to be an honest mistake?"

David's fingers bit down against the steering wheel. "Catarina never overreacts! I was a damned fool," he said tersely. "I should have opened the package then and there. I knew something was wrong."

Pengable Street was completely blocked off by emergency vehicles when David tried to turn onto it a few blocks north of the doll shop. They could see a plume of smoke rising thick against the sky from the rear of the old building. Petrina twisted around trying to keep the shop in sight as David parked.

"We'll leave the dolls in the trunk," he said. They hurried toward the shop on foot.

Julian was standing out in front, conversing with a uniformed policeman.

"What are you doing here?" he asked in surprise. "I thought you said your errand was planned for this noon."

"It was. Mr. Conolly mixed up the dolls," Petrina explained. "We were going back to exchange the one he gave me for the one I really chose."

Julian shook his head. "Afraid you won't be able to do that, pet. There was an incendiary that set all this off and most of the dolls are damaged by smoke and water. Even so, I can tell you that there was no other Pedlar doll. Lots of regular dolls. But none with trays and geegaws."

"Maybe I could talk with Mr. Conolly. He might have put it away for me." She knew from his expression what he was going to say, before he spoke, and she felt a little ill.

"Mr. Conolly was killed in the explosion, along with one of our undercover men who had the misfortune to be in the wrong place at the wrong time." He turned his face and coughed as the wind carried smoke and acrid fumes to him.

Petrina thought of the workman who had walked near them and listened to their conversation this noon. He might have been a policeman, intrigued by David's resemblance to Julian. She had no memory of the workman's face. Tears crowded into her eyes and she blinked hard.

"Take her out of here, Dave. Leave a message at my office and I'll get together with you later."

CHAPTER 8

"Would you like to come up with me for a while?" Petrina invited, when David pulled up to let her out in front of her hotel. "I'd rather not be alone right now."

His eyes softened as he looked up at her. "Give me time to find a spot for the bug. I'll be along directly."

Still numb with the horror of having stood close to sudden violent death, Petrina walked through the lobby mechanically, enclosed in a numbing protective cocoon of shock. She pressed the summons button at the side of the lift and when the door jolted open, stepped inside and rode up to her own floor.

After she had opened the door and stepped inside her room, she came alert with a chilling shock. The room was a shambles. The drawers of her dresser hung open like so many gaping mouths, contents jumbled about carelessly. Every inch of the area had been hastily and insolently ransacked. With a gasp of outrage she looked around, at dresses that had been shoved about, hatboxes pulled from the high closet shelf and dumped out on the floor, suitcases opened and searched.

The Colonel's carrying case had been emptied and the Colonel himself opened and his clothing pulled off before he had been tumbled unceremoniously into a corner. Nothing appeared to have been left untouched nor unturned.

In the bathroom her cosmetics evidenced the same

hasty but thorough examination. Cold cream had been stirred and explored, various cases opened.

She bent to pick up clothing from the floor and stopped herself. The police would want everything left as it was, she was sure, so that if there were any sense to be made of the violation they could make it. She pressed her trembling hands hard against her thighs and tried to regain control of herself. By the time David joined her she was ready to deal with the police.

David stopped short as he saw the extent of the mess then moved over to the dresser, the closet, the tray of cosmetics, stopped again. "What on earth could you have squirreled away here that could set off a search like this?" he asked in stunned wonder. "Or what could anyone think you might have?"

"Nothing." She flung out her arms in bewilderment. "Everything in my room has been picked over but I can't see that one thing is missing. Not one thing." She drew a deep ragged breath. "Would you leave a message at Julian's office and tell him that I'll wait here for him, David? And while you're doing that, I'll fix us a drink."

She heard him dialing as she reached up on the closet hat shelf and took down a bottle of Scotch she had kept there. "At least they left that alone." She rinsed out two glasses and poured in Scotch, then water at the bathroom lavatory, gave one glass to David. "I can ring for ice," she volunteered.

"This is fine," David assured. "We'd better not give any of the hotel help a look at the place until the police get here. No point in unnecessary agitation."

"Who would have done this? When?"

David shrugged and sipped his drink. "Some of it is hard to figure, isn't it? Somebody had to be sure something valuable—at least to them—was hidden in your room and to be determined to find it. But they had no idea of where to look. In fact, judging by this upheaval, they weren't quite sure what its appearance would be. That is the weirdest thing of all. As for when—all they had to do was watch your movements from the lobby and come up when you were out."

"It could have been someone on the hotel staff."

"Yes. It could." David finished his drink and walked over to fix himself another. His eyes were bleak. "This is one of the times when I wish I were capable of doing all the things the people in my audiences think I can."

Petrina took her drink over to the telephone. The call to Cypress Glade had to be made regardless of how much she preferred not to do it. At least she could call Sam Brock's law office and perhaps it would all end there.

"Are you afraid to talk to Tony?" David asked finally, as she waited for the overseas operator to call back. "Emotionally?"

"No!"

His eyebrows raised and she realized she had answered too quickly and too emphatically.

"I'm not afraid to talk to him. I just don't *want* to talk to him. There's a difference."

"Explain it to me." David leaned back lazily in the worn but comfortable chair beside a lamp table but his dark eyes were smoldering. "Since I never met him, I find it hard to understand his devastating charm—and he must have a considerable amount of it to have captivated both you and the perfidious Linette."

She was disturbed at the anger simmering beneath the surface of his remarks. He had never acted this way toward her about Tony before, not even back in Miami, when her broken romance was just about all she could talk about. He had been kind, then, had helped her build a new life, had listened.

Her own temper flared in response to his sarcasm. "This whole communication problem is all your fault so I can't see what you're complaining about," she accused sharply. "If you hadn't told Ken Evens he could give Linette my address, she wouldn't have been able to cable me. I wouldn't have known she had disappeared and I wouldn't be worried and calling for information." She glared at him. "I didn't intend to have anything to do with either one of them again."

The telephone rang and a few crackles later the overseas connection was made. She heard the smooth unctuous drawl of Linette's lawyer. Conscious of David's eyes on her, she was careful in her responses to the lawyer's opening remarks. She could almost see Sam Brock's heavy porcine face, flushed as it had been the day after Aunt Ellen's funeral, his small bloodshot eyes peering out with an expression that was at once arrogant and triumphant.

He had enjoyed reading her Aunt Ellen's will, which left the big house and the very large tract of land surrounding it as well as other acreage in and around Big Cypress to Linette. Most of Aunt Ellen's money had been left to Linette too, it turned out, clearly and explicitly stated in that fifteen-year-old will the lawyer brought from his safe after Aunt Ellen's death.

Remembering the malice in his eyes as he smiled over the will, Petrina's throat tightened. His glance lingered contemptuously on the tears that streaked her cheeks and his fat fingers drummed at the will as though he assumed she cried because she had received so little. He would not have been able to admit tears could be shed in grief and loneliness.

"This is an expensive call, Mr. Brock," she interrupted his flow of pleasantries. "And since I'm paying for it, I'd like to get to the reason I called. Has Linette been found yet?" When he started to launch into details of the search, she stopped him again. "Mr. Brock, please, just yes or no."

The line was silent for an instant. "No," he answered flatly, his voice suddenly hard and hostile.

"As Mr. Nairac told you last night, I received a cable from Linette telling me she needed my help and asking me to come home at once. Would you know why she might have sent that cable?"

Again there was silence. Sam Brock's voice held a thread of uneasiness when he answered, "No. Mrs. Addison has been pretty unstable the last few months and we haven't seen much of her. Mr. Addison has been taking care of her business affairs, with my help, of course. As far as possible. I don't know why she would cable you unless something set her off again."

"Again? She has disappeared before?"

"She always came back," the lawyer said defensively. "It was just for a day or two, once for a weekend."

Petrina drew a ragged breath. "And you say there are search parties out looking for her? She's been reported to Missing Persons?"

"Everything practicable has been done." The hostility had disappeared from his voice and it was quite conciliatory now. "I assure you, I'll call you immediately as soon as I hear anything. Good or bad, I'll telephone."

Slowly Petrina returned the telephone to its cradle.

"You felt there was something wrong there, didn't you?" she asked David. "You weren't satisfied with the answers you got from Sam Brock yesterday."

"No, I wasn't. Whatever is going on there, he isn't telling the truth about it."

She repeated what Sam Brock had said about Linette's emotional state. "She isn't an unstable type," Petrina said wryly. "Selfish, manipulative—but unstable just isn't her way of coping. She wouldn't run away, normally."

"But she *did* run away. And from the sound of it, she is determined to stay away, from her home and husband as well as everyone else."

"She's running scared," Petrina said slowly, "and there's no one she can turn to except me. No one she feels she can trust. I don't know what has happened to her but I do have to go to her and do what I can. She asked me to come home. If I do, how will she know I'm there?" Her heart began to thump. "David, would the theater give me leave to go home and look into the matter, do you think? Do they ever do that?"

He smiled kindly. "I can help with that, I think. Health and family emergencies are considered adequate reason for suspending a contract. I'll go with you to talk to Hugo Boyton, if you like. He and I are old friends. When you decide, we'll find a way."

Two men from Julian's office appeared at the door and David went on his way after arranging to pick her up for dinner around seven. The policemen stayed about an hour, carefully examining everything and trying vainly to raise possible fingerprints on the few surfaces that might have served to hold them.

After they had gone, Petrina showered and dressed, then settled down to vocal exercises and rehearsed a few routines. First she worked on resonances, the greater than normal resonance she used for Peter, arching her tongue and working on her throat movements and breathing. She hadn't used muffled or distant voice for a while so she practiced muffled consonants, especially sibilances, first, pushing her tongue down on the floor of her mouth until she was tired. Before she decided to call it a day she tried a few distant voice exercises too, a high hum, then the pushing back of tongue that sent nearly all the sound through her nose and created the distant note her father used to call a bee drone.

Keeping the distant voice was more bother than it was worth, there were so few places she played large enough for it to be used. This voice was impossible for small intimate clubs and the routines she was using with Peter didn't call for this vocalization.

Still, if Robert Gentry had kept it polished and in his formidable repertory, his daughter could do likewise. Who knew, it might come in handy one day. She caught sight of her gamin grin in the dressing table mirror, her hazel eyes gone almost a strange flecked blue, borrowing from the teal blouse and evening skirt she wore.

She wasn't sure she heard a knock at first but when it was repeated louder, she called out, "Who is it?"

"A message, miss." The accent was neither English nor American. She couldn't place it. It wasn't musical enough to be the Irish she was accustomed to hearing, either.

Petrina stiffened. "Slide it under the door," she directed.

"I have to have an answer, miss. Beg your pardon. It wouldn't take you but a minute."

"I'm not dressed to come to the door," Petrina invented, her voice chilly. "Either slide the message under the door or forget about it."

Her mind was racing as she waited. Why had he not reported at the desk downstairs and had a call made from there as was usual? How had he known her room number? The desk clerk would never have released it to him. Was he one of the ones who—

The edge of a white envelope became visible under the door and Petrina got hold of it and pulled it along. There was no name on the envelope. It had been meant to be hand-carried, personally delivered. She opened it and read the typed message.

"Dear Miss Gentry, The Pedlar dolls we bought at Mr. Conolly's doll shop were mixed by mistake. I have your doll. Mr. Conolly gave you mine. Since I'm sure we both prefer the doll we chose, may I ask that you select a place and time at your convenience and that we then exchange them? Thank you." There was no signature. No address.

"Are you still out there?" Petrina called out. No one answered. She heard the lift door jolt open down the hall, close, hum on its way. The safety chain was on the door. She resisted an impulse to open it and see if the messenger had gone. As slowly as the lift controls operated, someone could easily step inside, press a control button and step back outside again before the door closed and the lift moved.

A few minutes later she heard an almost inaudible soft curse outside her door and retreating footsteps, heavy even on the hall carpeting, and she leaned against the door, weak with reaction.

Someone really wanted that Pedlar doll, she thought, bewildered. Both dolls had been nice enough, but there were many Pedlars equal to them in quality and price and availability.

The gamin smile touched her lips again.

The doll wasn't even here. David still had the wrong Pedlar as well as Peter in the trunk of his black car. She frowned thoughtfully. Surely that search of her room could not have been an attempt to find and steal back a *doll*.

CHAPTER 9

Hugo Boyton's expression was noncommittal as he regarded Petrina across the expanse of his wide polished
desk top. Behind him heavy drapes were drawn to shut
out the distraction of early evening lights from the buildings and street beyond. The multicolored glow of his
Tiffany desk lamp cast a curious pattern of light and
shadow on his clever showman's face.

"A leave to attend to urgent personal matters in the
States?" he repeated her words. "Of course I would be
glad to accommodate you. On one condition."

She moved uneasily in the big comfortable leather
chair and glanced over at David for reassurance. His eye-
lid came down slightly in an all but imperceptible wink.

"I would like you to return and finish out your contract
as soon as you get things sorted out." Hugo Boyton abandoned his sternly considering manner and smiled broadly.
"Can't lose my investment in a fine performer, now, can
I?"

"She's that good?" David's question had a proprietary
flavor that seemed to amuse the theater manager.

"She's very good. She has the audience with her all the
way. Did you ever doubt it, David?" He threw back his
head and laughed aloud.

"Is Julian still mucking about backstage somewhere?"
David's question seemed casual enough, but the intent interest in his eyes weighted the query.

"With a team." Hugo Boyton's eyes no longer reflected

humor. His lips tightened. "I'm missing a dance team tonight—Morag O Cathan and Ben Downey—and I have a replacement control panel man tonight, regular called in sick." He stood up. "It's getting close to second evening performance and I'd better stand handy. I wish I knew what to expect."

"Don't we all." Petrina scooped herself out of the ample embrace of her leather chair. "Are you sure that I'm not letting you down tonight? I could very easily dress and be ready in time for my turn, and with Morag and Ben gone—"

"Thanks. I was able to get replacements with no trouble at all." He smiled. "Not as delightful as you, my dear, but I'll wait for my pound of flesh until you get back here from your trip."

A telephone rang in the outer office, the sound muffled by the thick door of the manager's office. After a brief indistinct acknowledgment, there was a tap on the door, then Nora Talson, the manager's secretary, looked in, her pert face alive with excitement.

"That was Commander Farr, sir. He just called from the lobby phone to say all is well. They located the incendiary and they have deactivated and removed it and taken a man into custody. The man who came in to take Dorsett's place at the backstage control panel."

Hugo Boyton took a deep breath. "Thank God. Is Dorsett down there?"

The secretary grinned. "He wants to know if he's entitled to keep the money he got as a bribe to report himself ill."

The manager shook his head and laughed. "He's entitled. To that and more. I'll settle with him after the show."

They walked out together, reaching the end of the corridor in time to see Julian shepherd his group through the lobby and out onto the steps leading down to the street. Julian paused as he caught sight of them, letting his men go on ahead with their prisoner.

The prisoner was the same man she had seen at the control panel with Morag, Petrina realized, and as the lobby began to fill with early arrivals for the night's second performance, she shivered with the chilling realization of what an incendiary set off in the theater could have meant.

"It was a little dicey there for a while," Julian admitted cheerfully. "Join me for a little celebration, David, Petrina? Anyone else?"

"Sorry, we'll have to pass it by." Hugo Boyton leaned down and planted an expansive kiss on Petrina's cheek. "If I don't see you again before your departure, *bon voyage*, love! Keep in touch!"

Julian rode with David. He had not had time to purchase an automobile of his own to replace the one that had been destroyed and his squad had already gone on with the department vehicle.

"I feel as though I'm between bookends," Petrina laughed, looking from David's profile to Julian's, so closely resembling it.

Julian loftily ignored her levity. "When do you leave, pet?"

"Tomorrow, if I can book a flight."

They settled down in a small cozy pub near her hotel for their nightcap. There had been some publicity about an innovation at the bar, a strip of polished metal so others in the room could be observed from the bar without unmannerly staring. The publicity was right. The whole room was visible without turning.

"Just as well you will be out of the city for a while," Julian said soberly, as they sipped their mild and bitters at the quiet saloon bar. "We aren't sure what is happening ourselves, anymore. There seems to be some internal struggle taking place in the terrorist hierarchy. Frankly, they would be doing us a big favor if they did dispose of one another, but I'm afraid that it won't be as neat as all that. Apparently Mr. Conolly was murdered in some of the infighting."

"Trina's dolls are still in the trunk," David said, remembering. "May as well leave them there until it's time to load you on the plane, little one. Let me know when you find out what flight you get and I'll take you out to the airport."

Petrina watched a party arrive and seat themselves at a table off against the wall, three men and a woman. The ribbon of polished metal attached to the bar reflected their faces so she could watch them without their knowledge.

They were arguing. Their voices rose in volume steadily until they realized they were attracting attention, then abruptly the sound damped. The spirited disagreement, however, continued.

Something about one of the male voices was familiar. Petrina watched the faces draw toward each other as the talk went on animatedly. In spite of the slight distortion of the mirroring surface, Petrina could see them clearly enough to be positive she did not recognize any of them.

It was the one male voice that she had recognized, she concluded finally, but she still could not place it.

Petrina became aware abruptly that the observation was mutual. The people at the table were closely scrutinizing David and Julian and her, too.

Suddenly the four stood up and without waiting to be served, moved swiftly toward the exit and out onto the street. The door swung shut and latched behind them.

Petrina turned back to Julian again, listening with divided attention. There had been another robbery in the

West End, this time some valuable art. It was too early for any of this loot to have been recovered. Nor had they had any leads on the priceless jewels stolen last week from a distinguished estate jeweler.

By this time tomorrow, she should be in Miami, Petrina thought. Perhaps Linette would have been found by then and there would be no need to talk to Tony and find that everything, or possibly, disastrously, nothing, had changed between them.

She felt David's eyes on her, dark and intent, and turned her thoughts to a safer subject, the party that had wandered in and so abruptly left again. David's eyebrows raised slightly, as though he were somehow aware of what she had done and why.

Soon afterward they left the pub themselves. The night air was cool and damp and there was a tang of salt in the breeze that swept in from the southeast. Petrina took a deep breath and looked down the street toward the neon flash of her hotel's illuminated sign. The wind lifted her hair and brought faint traces of voices from a passing automobile.

"What a beautiful night!" She stood at the open door of David's car.

"Pity it has to end," Julian agreed, waiting, not hurrying her.

She looked at the hotel sign again, reaching into her memory for some elusive connection that might identify the voice she had heard at the bar. Like the fragments from the passing automobile, that voice had been disembodied. A voice. Only a voice.

And then she had it. It was the voice of the man who had brought the message to her room. Though his voice had been muffled by the door in between, she had heard enough of the timbre and quality to have filed it away in her voice-trained mind for recognition another time.

Added to the voice itself was that final unmistakable factor, the accent. The accent that was not English, nor American, and possibly not Irish either—that was the speech pattern of the man who sat at the table near the wall observing them as closely as she had been observing him.

"You did recognize somebody back there, didn't you?" Julian asked softly. "I thought you might have."

"Just the voice," she replied shakily. "I remembered finally where I heard it, but it's too late to do any good. He was the man who pushed the message under my door at the hotel. I never saw his face."

Julian swore, apologized. "There was a rumor around the department that the terrorists had brought in someone from outside to tighten up their operation, robbery and fencing both. It's a small world. There was also a notice sent out a week ago that a first-class international thief had boarded a plane in Sydney, destination Paris. He arrived there but Sûreté Nationale reports he has disappeared. The Australians think he means to stay awhile in our part of the world. Do you believe your man might have been an Aussie, Petrina?"

"He didn't have the broad accent I associate with Australian speech. His speech was quite clipped, close to but not quite British. If some Australians talk like that, yes, he could have been."

Julian grinned tightly. "Some do, indeed. We've accomplished a good bit tonight, pet, figuring out what we have. David, do you suppose you could drop me off at New Scotland Yard before you take Petrina to her hotel?"

The cool innocence of the night air had disappeared. Petrina huddled back against the seat and after Julian had been left off began to tremble. David glanced over at her with concern.

"We'll be there soon, Trina."

He went up with her to her room and carefully checked it out, in spite of her protests, then pulled her suitcases down for her from her closet shelves.

At the door he paused and for a moment looked down at her, his eyes shadowed. "Best get your packing done tonight," he suggested. "Nora Talson should be able to get you space on a British Airways flight direct to Miami and that will give you a little more than seven hours' time to catch up on your sleep once you're aboard the plane."

"I wish I didn't have to go."

He ran a finger along the delicate line of her cheek. "So do I, Trina."

A shock of warmth moved along her skin at his touch and she lifted her face to his with surprise. He drew his hand away quickly and stepped back.

"I'll take you to the airport," he told her, his voice so matter-of-fact that she wondered if she had imagined the strange sensation of urgency he communicated. "Don't open your door to anyone and put on your chain latch after I leave." His eyes were still in shadow. "Good night, love."

She leaned dreamily against the door for a few moments after he had left and she had secured the door latch. With bemused interest she traced against her chin the same path David's finger had taken and thought about the surprised shock she had felt and about David's reaction, as though only by immediate return to the prosaic could he maintain his self-possession.

Something was changing in their relationship and she felt at once drawn and disturbed, exhilarated and depressed.

CHAPTER 10

The initial pink fingers of sunrise were reaching across the sky when Petrina closed the last of her packed suitcases. The Colonel's worn carrying case with the Colonel inside, his supercilious smile flattened against bent knees, huddled against a scuffed fortnighter plastered with travel stickers. Like an orderly island, the cluster of luggage had accumulated slowly in the middle of the room and now it was almost assembled.

Petrina's throat hurt suddenly and she swallowed but the hurt remained.

The room was picked bare of the scattering of personal things that had made it hers. Somehow, erasing signs of her occupancy here brought piercingly home the reality that she didn't want to leave this place where she had been very happy. She did not want to exchange her pleasant impersonal hotel room for space where her presence could not help but be resented. And she wanted no part of that old Victorian dwelling that Linette had inherited and in which she had made a home for Tony and herself.

For Petrina, home was as it always had been, luggage piled, ready and waiting to move with her from one place to another. She sighed bleakly. Back in Florida there was a little beach crab that wandered around under whatever empty shell suited his fancy, making a home that could be changed to accommodate circumstances. She might do worse than use the hermit crab as a model. Especially when she didn't have a whole lot of choice.

Her eyes grainy with gathering tears, she fell into bed for a few hours of sleep. Her eyes still felt gritty next morning when she awakened to the strident summons of the telephone bell.

The call was from Nora Talson, cheerful and efficient even at a distance. "You have a seat waiting for you on British Airways' flight to Miami leaving Heathrow at twelve forty-five."

"You're an angel." Petrina stifled a yawn and twisted around to check the alarm clock. "Good grief, Nora! It's nine o'clock!"

"Don't worry, pet! You have plenty of time." Nora laughed comfortably. "Let me tell you the rest. You'll be traveling club—that's midway between first class and economy. Lots of first-class perks and no economy drawbacks. Does that suit you? We can change it if you want."

"Don't change a thing. Where do I pick up my tickets?"

"No need. David just picked them up, along with your costumes and things from your dressing room. He's bringing it all to you."

"He's on his way here now?" Petrina shrieked.

Nora chuckled. "I thought that would put sparks in your eyes. *Bon voyage*, dear." Her voice was suddenly serious. "Take care and hurry back to us, won't you!"

As Petrina hurriedly showered and dressed, she found her spirits steadily rising. She pulled a soft green cashmere sweater over her head, smoothed a moss-green thin tweed skirt down over her slim hips and surprised a jaunty grin on the face that looked back at her from her dressing table mirror.

She was trying to subdue her rebellious hair into a satiny cap when David arrived with a porter in tow.

"Did Nora call you?" He looked her over approvingly and surveyed her stacked luggage with relief. "My car is down at the entrance. The porter and I will stow away your bags while you settle up at the desk. We can have coffee at the airport."

She left him supervising the loading up of the baggage cart and by the time the desk clerk had finished totting up her statement and she had made out her check, the bags were being trundled through the dim paneled lobby and out to David's waiting small black car. David's face was drawn and worried as he hurried her inside.

The brisk damp chill of morning wind through her open window brushed the last fuzz from Petrina's mind. She studied David's tense features as he drove swiftly through ferocious morning business traffic until finally they were humming along the flyovers and elevated motorway toward Heathrow.

Aware of her scrutiny, he ran a hand through his dark hair.

"You may as well tell me," she suggested.

"I would if there were anything to tell. That's the trouble." He swung out around a truck and pulled in behind a fast moving Bentley. "When I was at the theater this morning, a call came in from Morag's flatmate. Morag, it seems, was called away by sudden death in her family—someone else would dance her turn with Ben Downey until she could get back. The substitute will audition for Hugo and no doubt will be all right."

"Then as long as Hugo Boyton is satisfied, what is the problem?"

David's eyes narrowed against the road. "That's what bothers me, Trina. There should be no problem at all, now that she is gone, and yet there is. Morag has been involved with everything that was going on; her absence from here simply means that her base of operations has changed, that's all. She is still involved in the whole ugly business somewhere else. Julian has his reasons for being worried. My reason is you." He laughed ruefully. "There's no help for any of it, Trina. I'm glad you won't be here for a while, but I find, now we're down to the wire, that I don't like seeing you off for Florida alone, either."

"I'm glad."

"Are you?" His eyes rested on her momentarily, went back to the road.

For a moment she stilled, and her skin prickled as though it had been brushed by an invisible hand, gently, knowingly. As though the question he asked had entered her brain through her pores and was searching for its answer in her thoughts.

As suddenly as the feeling had come, it disappeared. Oddly bereft and disappointed, she settled back again.

The tense lines in David's face had eased. "Are you glad I don't want you in Florida alone?" he asked again, insistently, waiting for her answer.

"I told you I was."

David's lips twitched slightly with amusement. "I know. I wanted to hear it again." Behind his dark glasses his eyes were unreadable, fixed now on the road sweeping along above the roofs of Chiswick.

When they reached the vast complex of Heathrow David dropped her off, her bags piled around her, and roared away in search of a car park. As she upended one of her suitcases and perched on it, she watched the constant stream of vehicles roaring past, pulling up and disgorging passengers. She observed piles of bags similar to her own accumulate, watched porters swoop down and carry them off like ants at a sugar heap, watched the whole cycle repeat itself over and over again. Flight buses too dropped off their fares and she found herself examining passing faces as time elapsed and David had not yet reappeared.

And then, just as she caught sight of David approaching across the road with Peter's carrying case tucked under one arm and the Pedlar doll's package under the other, Petrina heard the voice of the Australian man from the midst of a party making its way toward the entrance from a flight bus pulled up just behind her.

Her eyes flicked over the faces of the men. She rejected two with full beards—the men last night at the pub were clean shaven—and passed by two dignified elderly gentlemen. She frowned as the others passed close without offering her any more interest than the appreciation extended any pretty girl on a sunny spring morning. In the bright sunlight she could not identify any particular face, and yet any one of them within a thirtyish range could have been the man she heard. And whoever he was, he must have seen her. She peered anxiously through the glass doors after them.

When David finally reached her, the load of passengers had scattered like blowing chaff to every direction in the great terminal and a new group had arrived on an enormous tour bus and was pouring out onto the unloading apron.

"You can carry Peter and the Pedlar on board with you," David informed her. "I checked the dimensions of Peter's case with the airline and the case will fit under the seat."

He put the repaired case down on top of a small trunk for support and opened it. Then he pulled off the wrapping from the Pedlar doll and removed the basket tray suspended from the doll's neck. Dexterously he slid the doll into the space that remained open beside Peter and laid the wares tray flat over both dolls, the tiny objects on the tray facing down and all of it held immobile by the snug fit once the top of the carrying case came down and was fastened.

After her luggage had been checked through they went into a restaurant and ordered coffee and Petrina told David about the voice she thought she recognized.

"You're sure about that?"

"Not positive. But reasonably sure. It couldn't matter, though. What would anyone do to me on a big aircraft?" She waited, but David remained silent. "Or in Miami or Cypress Glade?" He still didn't answer. "Why would they want to do anything?" She looked down at Peter's carrying case at her feet. "The only thing that man said he wanted was the Pedlar, but the Pedlar isn't worth the kind of trouble he's gone to. A three-hundred-dollar doll! Even if it is the wrong one. If he'd wanted to exchange that badly he could have made another effort and done it in a more conventional way. I'd be glad to exchange. I prefer my own doll anyhow!"

David signaled for more coffee. "That worries me. That they haven't made another try for the doll, if they really want it. Nothing makes any sense. But I'm asking you to be careful, Trina. Rent yourself a car when you get to Miami and get on out to Cypress Glade. You can stay at Linette's house for the time being. I'll telephone you there tonight."

"How about 'don't talk to strange men' and—"

David's face flushed with anger. "This is no joke, Trina."

She regarded him soberly. "No, David, it isn't. Not any of it."

For a moment his dark eyes held her. He moved his hand in a gesture of apology. "Sorry. I'm jumpy. I have no business doing the take-charge bit." He checked his watch. "Finish up, if you want any more of that coffee. It's time to get you checked in."

The London-to-Miami flight took off on schedule. Petrina sat back in the comfortable gold embrace of her seat and closed her eyes as she listened to the announcements, opened them for the demonstration of oxygen masks and safety instructions and kept them open while the plane reached for altitude.

As the English countryside west of Heathrow dropped out of sight and the blue Atlantic took its place, she tried not to think ahead. Not about Linette and what might have happened by now. Not about Tony.

Her seatmate stirred and his shin bumped the edge of Peter's carrying case, protruding slightly from underneath her seat.

"Would you like me to put it up out of the way in the locker for you?"

Petrina had just closed her eyes for a nap. She sighed and opened them again. "I'm sorry you were inconvenienced," she apologized, and for the first time really looked at the rotund little man who had slipped breathlessly into his seat just before the plane took off.

He was a clergyman, she saw with surprise, an Episcopalian or possibly a Roman Catholic by the look of his white collar.

"I hope you weren't hurt, Father." She pulled the case out and handed it to him and watched as he wrestled it up into the overhead locker directly above their seats. He grasped the locker cover and snapped it down.

"Thank you."

"Glad to help." Bright blue eyes twinkled youthfully from a middle-aged face. "You can see plainly what my occupation is, young lady, but may I ask what you do in the world?"

They chatted through a drink and placed their orders for dinner. Father Wooster was returning to Florida from a visit to an English friend he had made when they were both chaplains in Korea, Father Wooster with a paratroop unit there.

Petrina was grateful for the wide-ranging conversation that diverted her from what lay ahead.

"It must be very different for you, pastoring a church in a small Florida town after the more exciting ministries you've had," Petrina said.

"Not at all," Father Wooster chuckled. "We have some exciting things going on in our part of the Everglades, too. A flock and the human condition always have a way of adding up to the unexpected and problematical."

After dinner was served they watched a movie for a while but Petrina's eyes grew heavy and she relaxed and slept feeling oddly secure with Father Wooster sitting solidly beside her, his bright eyes fixed on the screen, his muscles responding involuntarily to the action going on in the story.

She wasn't sure how long she had been asleep when she became aware of a disturbance near the divider separating the economy section from club.

"Sir, you are traveling in the economy-class cabin," she heard a stewardess say courteously but with cool authority. "You should not really go up into the club-class cabin."

"I wanted to see if an acquaintance of mine was on the plane."

Petrina stiffened and came alert at the sound of that male voice. He was on this aircraft, the Australian she had noticed at Heathrow.

"Sorry. I'll return to my cabin, of course."

She turned in time to see a back disappear past the curtains and into the tail portion of the aircraft.

"Problem?" The clergyman's eyes were concerned and he removed his headset.

"No, I don't think so." But Petrina knew the color had drained from her face and she shivered. "I believe I'll have a glass of brandy, though. In coffee."

She sipped from the cup, too disturbed to close her eyes again, even though she knew she was perfectly safe here beside the portly priest. He did not pry, but she was aware of his attention and speculation as he opened the magazine he drew from his briefcase.

Nothing would happen, she thought, until the plane landed at Miami. Whatever the Australian wanted, it would have to wait until they had landed and gone through customs. Until she had left the air terminal and its bustling activity and set forth, alone and vulnerable.

They landed in Miami at four-fifty, after a little more than seven hours in the air, and as always Petrina was bemused by the mathematics of time zones as she set her watch to Eastern Daylight Savings Time from British Summer Time.

The dreary walk from airplane to customs led up and down assorted flights of stairs and through long corridors past directional signs almost impossible to find. In the end each tired passenger seemed to settle for trudging in the wake of each preceding soul, too cowed or too traumatized to adventure into independent search.

At last the trail ended with a huge room filled with long tables and customs attendants. Across the hall Petrina sighted a rumbling gondola endlessly presenting its collection of baggage to be snatched away or circled around and presented again.

Petrina gathered up her luggage from the gondola and piled it on a carrier, along with Peter's case, wedged near the top. She queued up and felt Father Wooster's hand touch her arm diffidently.

"I'd suggest the next line," he said softly. "Behind that Asian gentleman. I've noticed they always check the Asians and the Colombians particularly thoroughly. They go over their things so carefully that the line becomes backed up quite a bit and the next ones following go through pretty fast. I shall be joining the third line down, myself."

Petrina joined the line he suggested, amused to see that his analysis was absolutely correct.

"Have you anything to declare?" the customs officer asked her.

She opened the case containing the Colonel and produced the receipt for him as well as for the Pedlar, both exempt because they were antiques. Her Equity card simplified explaining her possession of Peter and the collection of costumes and the examination procedure was soon completed.

As she turned to assemble her luggage on a carrier again, she found herself momentarily facing the table to her left. Lying there on the table, its bright clothing billowing out around it, lay a Pedlar doll. She froze, her eyes raising from the doll to the man who stood beside it, lifting his flight bag to the table.

He inclined his head in ironic recognition.

"Have you anything to declare?" the customs officer inquired of him.

Petrina turned away and finished loading her things as he replied. It was the Australian and he knew exactly who she was. But one thing was different now. She knew who he was, too, and what he looked like. Her wide eyes had registered every detail, the thin wind-dried face with its narrow mocking eyes, the lips pressed into a hard flat line, the wiry athletic tension of his angular body.

CHAPTER 11

Father Wooster was finished at customs at about the same time as Petrina so they walked out together to the automobile rental counter, a skycap trailing along with their substantial accumulation.

As Petrina pulled a rental questionnaire across the counter to fill it in, she glanced at her watch. It was almost six o'clock already, Miami time.

"Did you intend to drive all the way to your parsonage tonight?" she asked Father Wooster. "The way I juggle the arithmetic of it, it would be eleven o'clock tonight for us if we were still back in London—and it's been a long day. I'm going to stay over at a motel and start out for the Glades tomorrow morning early, myself."

"Your plan has considerable merit," Father Wooster agreed. "There is no point in driving half asleep, is there?"

Petrina caught sight of the Australian emerging from a corridor across the waiting room and suddenly what had begun as a vague idea became a practical option. She did not want to be wandering Miami alone tonight, nor traveling the dark deserted reaches of Alligator Alley across the Glades alone either, tonight or tomorrow.

"Father, I could drop you off at a motel, if you want to stay over too. I'd be glad to pick you up tomorrow morning and you could ride with me to Cypress Glade. You might call your parsonage from there and have somebody come for you."

His shrewd bright eyes narrowed slightly as he considered. "I see. All right, and thank you, Miss Gentry. And since you are saving my flock the price of an automobile rental to get their pastor back again, supposing I thank you by inviting you to dinner?"

"Done," Petrina agreed. "If I can pay my own way."

"You're a hard trader, Miss Gentry," Father Wooster observed. "I concede. On condition that you allow me to attend to having our bags moved out to the front pickup zone while you find your vehicle and bring it around. Without," he added sternly as she opened her mouth, "arguing with me about sharing the tip."

She handed her credit card to the clerk, who checked over her application form. In a few minutes she stood with her set of car keys and directions for finding the vehicle. Father Wooster waited expectantly.

"You win."

He nodded. "It happens now and then. Not as often as I might wish." He was signaling a skycap as she hurried across the crowded lobby.

After picking up the compact she had selected and checking her gas, she returned to gather Father Wooster at the terminal entrance. He stowed all of her bags away in the trunk and settled his own in the back seat, but he seemed preoccupied, although he didn't speak until they were pulling up in front of a modest restaurant near the airport.

"Miss Gentry, I think we'd better have a talk," he suggested, making no move to get out of the car.

"All right." Petrina was puzzled, but she assumed his talk had to do with their arrangements to pay for dinner.

Instead Father Wooster fixed her with a sharp appraising gaze. "I do not mean to pry into your business on short acquaintance, my dear, but I must put you on notice that I am not a fool, either. I observed your uneasiness at seeing one of our fellow passengers, on the airplane and later at the terminal. I think you should know that after you left to secure this car, the man went to the car rental desk himself to ask for an automobile. Before the clerk could file your application away, he picked it up and read it."

"Then he knows where to find me," Petrina said through stiff lips. "I gave Cypress Glade as my billing address. He'll have no trouble locating me there, if that is what he wants to do."

"You'd best lock up this car," the clergyman said, getting out. "I intend to inflict myself on a clerical friend of mine tonight and I prefer not to have to borrow his pajamas because my bags were stolen in a restaurant parking lot."

She realized that he was trying to distract her, now that he had dropped his bombshell, and was touched by his effort. He trotted along beside her, his body moving with an athletic strength and smoothness that belied both his age and his weight. On the plane he had mentioned his service as a chaplain to paratroopers in Korea. Paratroop chaplains trained with their troops and his muscles had not forgotten what they had learned in years past.

He held the door open for her.

When they had been seated, she leveled a straight challenging glance at him. "I want you on my side, Father," she said. "I'm going to tell you all I know about that man."

She had told him a great deal more than she had intended by the time they worked their way through an unexpectedly good red snapper dinner and a really memorable slice of cherry cheesecake and coffee. Father Wooster listened intently without comment until she had finished.

"First the man tried to exchange dolls with you, then

he made no further effort. As though there had been some basic change of plan."

"And he is here now with the other doll." Petrina turned toward their waitress. "Separate checks, please."

"At least he isn't following you now," the clergyman said. "He was still busy making his arrangements at the terminal desk when we left."

"He doesn't have to follow me, does he?" Petrina said grimly. "He knows where to find me."

She marked time while Father Wooster telephoned his friend, then dropped him off at the parish house of a church tucked into the run-down outskirts of town, promising to return for him at seven the next morning.

A reasonably respectable motel flashed its vacancy sign a few blocks down on a nearby business street and she pulled in at the office, too tired to search further.

Only an overnight case went with her into her room, set at the end of the sprawling building. She left the rest of her luggage in the trunk of her car and backed it into its parking slot so she could hear if anyone tampered with the catch during the night. Father Wooster's apprehensions about theft rubbed off, she thought ruefully.

Before she undressed to shower and get ready for bed, she tried to call David to tell him she had arrived safely. He would have finished at the theater by now so she placed her call to his hotel. When he did not answer, she called Julian's office finally and left a message for him there with Julian's assistant, who happened to be in.

Jet lag caught up with her abruptly and she was asleep almost as she straightened out on her bed.

Morning found her revived, her thoughts in order as they had not been the night before. She dressed hurriedly and packed her overnight case, eager to check the rental car and only too aware that it could have been towed away intact for all she could have known or prevented.

She thrust her key into the trunk lock and breathed a sigh of relief as she saw everything in order.

At a little past seven she pulled up in the driveway of the parsonage where she had left Father Wooster, tooted the horn twice. He came out promptly and tossed his bags into the back of the car. His eyes were heavy and red-rimmed and it was obvious he had spent his evening enjoying his old friend rather than catching up on his rest.

Petrina smiled. "Where do we pick up Alligator Alley?"

"You'll find twenty-seven a few blocks west of here. Take it north until we get to the toll plaza and head west." He let his head fall back against the back of the seat and closed his eyes.

After she had driven several blocks she asked, "Do they call it Okeechobee Road, too?"

"They do." He did not bother to open his eyes.

"Then I know it. Is it all right with you if we wait to have breakfast until we get to Cypress Glade?"

"I'd be pleased." He sighed.

Traffic was moving along quickly going north and soon Dania Reservation with Okalee Indian Village came up to the east, passed, and shortly afterward she moved through the toll plaza and onto Alligator Alley. She watched the other traffic for the first few miles, anxiously examining the occupants of each car that passed her, checking the rear-vision mirror every time a car stayed behind her for any length of time.

At last she settled back as the traffic thinned and steadied. There was no point in pressing for speed. She would be in Cypress Glade soon enough. There was no use anticipating what she might find there, either. Good or bad, she would learn what had happened soon enough, too.

On either side stretched a blurred changing tapestry,

the sheen of water through saw grass, the sparse elegant brush strokes of pine and cypress against the brightening morning sky. She began to wish she had chosen the Tamiami Trail instead, with its more interesting progress past the top of Everglades National Park, through the lower part of Big Cypress Swamp and at least a few settlements here and there.

Alligator Alley cut through the middle of Big Cypress Indian Reservation, then began to traverse the eastern portion of Big Cypress Swamp.

Petrina was aware suddenly of Father Wooster's intent scrutiny.

"So you're awake now, are you?" she jeered. "Some entertaining passenger you are."

He was checking the rear-vision mirror. "You haven't picked up company, I take it?"

"No problem." She caught his sidelong glance. "I know, Father. I know. Not yet."

A half-hour later she saw the sign for their exit ramp and came off the isolation of the toll road and onto the connecting road that cut its paved swath through the primordial vegetation and animal population of Big Cypress Swamp.

It wasn't far to Cypress Glade now. Petrina rolled down her window and breathed deep the magic odor of water and trees, of countless small plants blooming profusely out across the green reaches of the swamp.

"My God, imagine her being out there by herself," Petrina said, her voice thin. "Father, do you think my cousin could be lost out there and still be alive?"

The clergyman did not answer. He, too, was looking off to the distances to be seen.

Petrina's hands tightened on the steering wheel. "She did most of her growing up here," she said. "She knows the country well."

She watched for a gravel road off to the right, made a turn. Alongside the road there soon appeared a small collection of business places, a filling station, a country store with a post office sign in its window, several concrete-block buildings with professional signboards and a scattering of houses that wandered back among the trees. Petrina followed the road out of town to where it became a dirt road covered with a topping of crushed limestone.

Another turn, onto a narrower private road, over a culvert that spanned an intrusion of slough and suddenly there it was, the silvery gray cypress towers and wide verandas of Aunt Ellen's house rising from the hammock on which it had been built like some dream construction produced from the miasma of the swamp itself.

Petrina heard Father Wooster's sharp intake of breath. "It has a strange charm, hasn't it?" she remarked, but her eyes were on several cars parked closely to the side of the veranda. She pulled in beside them and turned off her ignition.

Had a search party just returned? She pushed the door latch and stepped out stiffly, grateful that Father Wooster was following suit.

She saw the front door open and Tony stood there, tall and blond, his gray eyes wide with shocked surprise at the sight of her. And fear? Was it possible that the shadow that darkened them momentarily was fear?

He recovered quickly and came forward down the steps, his arms open for an embrace she avoided by drawing Father Wooster to her side.

"Has Linette been found?" she asked, her voice ragged with the tumult of emotion that rocked her at the sight of him.

"No."

He looked over at Father Wooster and she made an introduction and explained the clergyman's presence. With hospitality forced upon him, Tony invited, "Come on into the house. You too, of course, sir," as Father Wooster hesitated. "I'll see that your bags are brought in shortly, Trina. You'll be staying here, naturally, in your old room."

He led the way into the large living room she remembered from the old days, colorful now with Linette's bright floral choices covering the furniture Aunt Ellen used to have upholstered in sticky velvet. Overhead a big flat-bladed fan softly churned the warm air. Several men stood up as she followed Tony through the door. She stopped short, her heart pounding in her throat as one of them smiled in recognition.

"Miss Gentry," he said. "We meet again." It was the Australian.

CHAPTER 12

"What are you doing here?" Petrina demanded, aware of the clergyman's hand pressed in warning against her elbow, but pushing aside its message of caution. Rash with the anger that followed her initial shock at finding the Australian here before her, waiting for her, she faced him with defiant challenge. "How dare you follow me?"

His narrow eyes gleamed knowingly and he let her see his pleasure at having outmaneuvered her. "But I didn't follow you here, Miss Gentry. As you may not have noticed, I was here when you came."

Tony moved uncomfortably. "Mr. Tyron came here this morning asking where you might be reached, Trina. I had just finished telling him you were in London, last I'd heard." His voice took on a note of petulant complaint. "Really, you should have sent word. I didn't expect you."

Petrina ignored him. She would deal with him later. She pinned the Australian with continued irate concentration. "What do you want with me, Mr. Tyron?"

"I came to exchange the dolls that Mr. Conolly, God rest his soul, mixed when he sold them to us. I'm sure you'd prefer the doll you chose, and I know that I want my own doll back. Indeed I do." His words were soft and conciliatory but in the hardness of his eyes was an unmistakable threat. "So let's get on with the trade. I have a customer who is waiting for it."

Petrina stiffened. There had been times when she had wanted nothing more than to exchange the dolls that had been responsible for so many difficulties. But with those narrowed menacing eyes on her, she blazed with perverse wrath. He was *not* going to harass her and intimidate her, to bully her into compliance with his wishes. She might indeed end up exchanging dolls with him, but if so, it would be when she chose, not when he dictated.

"It's too bad that you've gone to so much effort and expense to run me down, Mr. Tyron," she told him coldly. "I do have in my possession a doll I bought from Mr. Conolly. I intend to keep it. I also have the receipt he gave me which proves I purchased it—if it becomes necessary to produce it."

"You know you have the wrong doll." His voice was harsh and lashing for an unguarded instant.

"No," she answered him positively. "I know no such thing. I just know that you seem to want my doll and that you've spent a great deal more on a plane ticket, even traveling economy, than the doll is worth."

Seeing his hands clench into white-knuckled brutal fists at each side, Petrina knew that had she been alone, those fists would have been used to punish her and to force her into submission.

"It is obvious the lady does not wish to deal with you, Mr. Tyron," Father Wooster's voice said crisply, in back of her. "I suggest you accept that fact as gracefully as possible and leave."

The Australian pulled himself into a semblance of self-possession only by keeping his eyes away from both Petrina and the clergyman. "I'll give you time to think things over," he said, picking up the parcel he had brought with him. His lips were drawn so tightly across his teeth that he had difficulty speaking. "I suggest that you do use the time to consider my offer very seriously. My customer wants his property back and he does not intend to take no for an answer."

Petrina's eyes widened as she watched him standing with his parcel, remembering that parcel open on the customs table. "Something just occurred to me, Mr. Tyron. Did you have a particular reason—"

"No, Miss Gentry!" the clergyman broke in sharply.

"Let the lady talk," the Australian said softly. "I find what she is saying very interesting."

Suddenly frightened, Petrina looked about the room, at Tony standing bewildered and uneasy, at the other three men, two in business suits, one in rough camp clothes, watching the scene with objective interest, at the Australian and Father Wooster.

"Did you have a reason for letting me carry the wrong doll through customs, while you carried the other?" Petrina completed the question she wished she hadn't begun. She heard a sharp indrawn breath but she didn't know who drew it.

"Would you care to be more explicit?" the Australian asked with deadly politeness.

"Not right now." Petrina faced him squarely. "Perhaps after I have a chance to think things over, as you intimated earlier. Where can I get in touch with you, Mr. Tyron?"

He regarded her from those narrow eyes. "I'll get in touch with you, Miss Gentry. A week from today. Do you intend to be here that long?"

Tony stepped forward, his hand outstretched in a grotesque parody of a polite host. "I'm sure that if there is some change in her plans we will have a forwarding address," he offered. When the Australian made no attempt to shake hands, Tony let his arm drop.

"Good-by," Petrina said with a firmness that used up the last of her composure.

"I'll be back, Miss Gentry. Depend on it."

Nobody spoke as the sound of his heels echoed along

the hallway and foyer, stopped at the door, continued sharply across the wide porch and down the front steps. A car roared to life, snarled away from the parking area, went swiftly down the drive and off in the distance.

Tony mopped his forehead and sat down abruptly. "My God, Trina, what were you trying to do? You practically accused the man of using you to smuggle something through customs! What is this all about?"

"Perhaps I'll tell you another time, Tony, though it really is none of your business. Sorry."

Affronted, he opened his mouth to retort and couldn't, apparently, find words.

A slow grin moved across the face of the man dressed in camp gear. "Is this your wife's cousin?" he asked Tony. "Sam Brock said she was in London."

A new kind of tension crept into the atmosphere.

"I'm Linette's cousin," Petrina answered for herself. "Are you men from the search party that has been looking for her?" She paused uncertainly. The men in business suits had obviously not been very far from the protection of office or their automobile this morning.

"As a matter of fact, no." The man in camp clothes was amused by something of which the others seemed to be aware. "We are searching, but not for the missing lady." The amusement left his face. "There are plenty of people a lot more experienced than we are at hunting missing people who are looking for her out there."

"I'm glad," she retorted tartly, "since Tony doesn't appear to be stirring the saw grass too strenuously."

For the second time she saw a flash of fear cross Tony's eyes, suppressed immediately. "Linette has been missing for a week," he defended himself. "I have been out there with the sheriff's party for days on end, Trina. A man has to rest, too."

Father Wooster settled himself comfortably in one of

the flowery big chairs. "Please excuse my staring," he said affably, "but I feel I have seen you men before. Aren't you with one of the oil companies operating wells in Big Cypress south of Immokalee? One of my parishioners pointed you out when you were negotiating with him about a lease on land he owned."

"We did some exploratory work up that way," one of the businessmen said, without hesitation. "I don't remember meeting you, though, Father, and I seldom forget a face."

The clergyman nodded with satisfaction. "Nor I, sir. We did not meet. My parishioner merely identified you to me as you passed on the street." He turned to Tony. "Might I use your telephone, please? I'd like to call my parish house over in Annona Township. Collect, of course."

Tony showed him into the adjacent study and returned to the living room quickly, before conversation had a chance to develop among the four left there. The three oil men exchanged glances that apparently were a signal.

"We can hold off for a while," the man in a light-gray suit said softly, "but as you can understand, not indefinitely. We have to run our exploratory wells before we know whether there is anything to be taken from the area and we cannot take the first step until the legal situation is secure. But of course you know all that. Please let us know the instant you hear from your wife." His level eyes considered Tony. "Or about her." His chilling implication was plain.

Tony nodded.

The man's gaze shifted to Petrina momentarily and confirmed what she surmised, that he had deliberately informed her of their business here, knowing that Tony would have no intention of doing so. The three left a few minutes later.

"I'll see that your things are carried up to your room right away," Tony volunteered. "May I have the keys to your trunk, Trina?" He took them and started out of the room, then paused. "Have you had breakfast yet? Would you like something?"

Father Wooster returned to the room before she could answer, his telephone call completed. "I can't speak for Miss Gentry, but speaking for myself, I would very much like something to eat. We left so early this morning we did not take time to breakfast."

After Tony had gone about his errands, the clergyman glanced about the room with interest. "This is a most unusual house to find around here," he commented. "Something this elaborate and elegant."

"Linette inherited it from my aunt," Petrina explained. "My uncle logged out enough timber from his holdings in Big Cypress back in the forties to make himself a very rich man and he built this house for her. They had a house in Miami too, but when his health failed, they rented out the house in the city and lived out here. The city house finally turned into a roominghouse. It was in Linette's estate so it's still hers, unless she's sold it. My uncle and aunt used up most of the really big money before he died but Aunt Ellen had enough to live on nicely and she never sold an acre of their land, either here or around Immokalee and Okeechobee."

The clergyman's face still registered puzzlement. "I thought I knew most of the history of the old-timers in this part of the state but I don't remember the name Gentry from around here."

"My father was an entertainer," she said. "A ventriloquist. Robert Gentry."

Comprehension lighted his eyes. "Of course! I knew the name Gentry was familiar but I didn't reach back far enough to make the connection."

"My uncle's name was Ezekiel Stafford. The Staffords were an old Okeechobee family and he was the last of it. They called him E.Z. around here, as though the initials were a nickname."

The startled look on Father Wooster's face had changed as she spoke to alert interest. For a while he sat in silence, clearly turning the information over in his mind.

"I never met your uncle or aunt," he said. "I arrived in Annona after he had died and my work never took me down this way. But I have heard about E.Z. Stafford and his passion for land. A vast empire of it, I hear. So it was left to your cousin Linette, was it? That doesn't sound like a very fair thing to do."

"Mr. Brock, her lawyer, said it was because Linette was like a daughter to her. Oh, what does it matter? It's done and past. Nothing can be changed and I don't really care."

"May I ask the date of the will? Do you remember?"

She shook her head impatiently. "It was many years prior to the time I came here to live. Mr. Brock drew the will up for her and kept it in his office safe, as so many lawyers do. After she died he handled the details. I was left several thousand dollars which were deposited to my account in the bank I use in Miami."

"She didn't write another will after you came here to live and she got to know you? I find that very strange. I can see that she might not have felt an undue consideration toward a niece that she hardly knew—but that situation would have changed entirely once you came here. She was a businesswoman and a fair woman, from anything I've heard. I can't see her arranging anything this inequitable."

Petrina shrugged. "She spoke of writing another will— but she must never have gotten around to it. She could see I was started on my own career in show business. Perhaps she thought I wouldn't need the money."

"I wonder if you have any idea what kind of money you might be talking about," the clergyman speculated mildly.

"Thousands of acres of swampland?" She laughed with honest amusement. "I know that oil has been found in various areas of Big Cypress, but the Stafford holdings have been a long way from the big finds!"

"You might look into the matter before you take that for granted," the clergyman advised. "Something doesn't compute here."

"For a man of the cloth, you have a very materialistic attitude," she reproved.

"Realistic," he corrected. "I need to have in a parish as poor as mine." He got up and peered down the hallway. "It's been mighty peaceful and quiet back there for people who are supposed to be getting breakfast for a couple of starving guests. I heard the car being unloaded and the suitcases going up the stairway but I do not hear the beguiling clanks of skillets nor do I smell the aroma of coffee and toast and whatever."

Petrina laughed. "I'll go and investigate."

She glanced out of the front door and saw her car standing neat and unattended, its trunk closed. Then she followed the hallway back to the capacious kitchen with a modern range set into the cupboarding, that was new, and a new tall deepfreeze unit—a whole array of shining new appliances in lemon yellow standing on a new flagstone floor of gleaming Spanish tile. But not only were there no preparations for breakfast in progress, there was no sign of anyone at the back of the house to attend to the cooking.

From the ceiling . overhead came a faint creak of

boards. Petrina opened the door to the back stairs that led up from the big pantry and cautiously began to climb them, moving carefully so the old treads would not betray her. When she reached the top of the stairs she oriented herself, locating the origin of the sound she had heard, and was not surprised to find that it had come from her old room.

She opened the door and surprised Tony leaning over the opened case that held Peter and the Pedlar doll. He had the Pedlar doll clasped in his hands and was squeezing the body of it, hard.

"Just what do you think you're doing?" she demanded fiercely.

Tony dropped the doll back into the case. "The lid came open as I was putting it down and I was curious."

You said you were going to have the bags carried up, not that you were going to do it yourself. Where is Ira? Where is his wife? Don't they work here anymore? Nobody was in the kitchen."

"Ira is out with the search party. Sara quit after Linette disappeared and then I heard she had hurt her foot. I was going to tell you about them but I didn't want to go into all that with that clergyman sitting there. What would he think?"

"Probably the same thing I am," she returned tartly. "That you are lying and I wish I knew how much and about what. You really did think there was something valuable smuggled through customs in that doll, didn't you?"

"Miss Gentry! Is everything all right?" Father Wooster called up the front stairwell.

"I'll be right down." Petrina stood at the door and waited until Tony left the room. Then matter-of-factly, making no attempt at concealment, she took the old-fashioned key out of the inside door lock and locked the door behind her from the outside while Tony stood waiting.

Tony watched her, his body pulled defensively up to its full height. "You didn't have to do that."

"I'm glad you told me," Petrina returned derisively. "It makes me feel no end better."

"You misunderstood what I meant." His eyes were unreadable. "It's just that several of the keys in this house fit other locks. Your door has a lock like that."

CHAPTER 13

As she emerged from the pantry stairwell into the big bright kitchen, the full impact of her situation struck Petrina. With Sara gone and Ira off on a search party, she would be alone with Tony here at the house, once the clergyman left. She stumbled and felt Tony's hand on her arm, balancing her. With quick revulsion she jerked away.

"Don't panic," Tony jeered with malicious amusement. "So it's finally come to you that there will be just the two of us here together, has it? There are worse things than being alone with me, Petrina, if you just think about it. You used to tell me how you could hardly wait for the time when we could be alone, you know."

Her eyes widened with shocked distaste. She felt as though her thoughts were visibly chasing themselves across her hazel eyes, and from the tightened muscles at either side of his mouth she knew that he was fully aware of her feelings and that he was affronted by them.

What might have happened if the clergyman had not been standing clearly in view, regarding them with thoughtful interest? Or if he were not there at all? She would have to think about that and quickly.

"When will your housekeeper be here to pick you up?" Petrina asked Father Wooster, casually, as though it didn't really matter, but her voice was thready, a little too high.

"About a half hour from now at most. It shouldn't take

that long. I'm adding a little for traffic and getting the old truck started and a half dozen kids in the front yard who might want to come along and can't." His eyes creased happily at the corners. "They act as though I'm back from a dangerous adventure when I drive over to Naples by myself, and that's only forty miles. You can imagine how they must feel about my coming back from England."

Tony walked over to the big refrigerator and removed a box of eggs, a loaf of bread and a package of sausages from the interior. He peeled the sausages off into a skillet and cracked several eggs into a bowl without consulting his guests for preferences on how they might like to have them prepared.

"This won't be fancy." Tony began to beat the eggs.

Petrina opened the loaf of bread and dropped two slices into the toaster. When they had browned she dropped in two more. "Are you eating with us, Tony?"

"I'll have coffee with you. I had my breakfast earlier." His expression mocked her. "Thank you."

She set the table while the food was cooking, poured coffee, finally portioned out the cooked sausage and scrambled eggs. Father Wooster tied into his allotment with hearty gusto but his thoughtful eyes were attentive to something more serious than food. She observed his gaze fasten repeatedly on Tony in assessment. She had hoped to have at least a few moments to confer with the clergyman before he left but when she heard the sound of an ancient pickup approach down the road, she had a feeling time had run out.

Father Wooster cocked his head as the truck sound lumbered closer. "She got it going," he approved. "When I talked to her she wasn't sure it would even turn over."

Tony came to his feet deliberately and his eyes met Petrina's with mocking question, aware as she was of her difficult choices. She could remain here alone with him at whatever jeopardy to her own reputation and her relationship with Linette, not to mention the physical threat that Tony openly suggested. Or she might desert the field and retreat to the safety of Father Wooster's parsonage.

"After you, Miss Gentry." The clergyman pulled her along toward the hall, temporarily securing her a reprieve. "We can't have the lady decide I am not here and go off to the village to find me." He chuckled at the sound of vigorous banging on the heavy timber of the front door. "She is a very determined lady, my good Miss Marinta."

He hurried along and threw the door open in the midst of another barrage of blows. "Come in, Miss Marinta!"

Through the door strode an enormous black woman, her face radiant with delight. "It's good to have you back, Father!" The clergyman and his housekeeper exchanged a quick glance and she nodded, in answer to a silent question. "No trouble about it. My sister was able to come."

Father Wooster turned beneficently to Tony. "I have very good news for you. I was aware that you might have a problem with your wife gone, sir, and even out this far from society people sometimes conjecture and gossip whether there is cause or not. So when I telephoned the parsonage, I asked Miss Marinta if she might be able to get her sister to take her place with me while she came here to stay as long as you might need her. I didn't want to risk disappointment by telling you of my idea until I ascertained that it would work out."

A wave of shattering relief swept over Petrina, leaving her weak.

Tony stood rigid and silent, his face livid.

"I put my suitcase right out there on the porch," Miss Marinta said. "You think you can get that truck back to

Annona by yourself, Father?" Apparently this was a joke because they both guffawed heartily.

"I almost ran it into an Okeechobee canal once and got a ticket for reckless driving," the clergyman explained to Petrina.

She had carefully avoided turning in Tony's direction, afraid of meeting his eyes, but she jerked around as he slammed his fist against the wall.

"I'm not paying for a housekeeper I didn't hire," he snapped harshly. "You can get her out of here. Right now."

"I'll pay her salary," Petrina said hurriedly. "And there's plenty of room for her. She can use the bedroom next to mine, Linette's old room." She blinked away a prickling of tears of gratitude as she held the clergyman's hands in hers for a moment. "Thank you. Thank you very much."

"I'll need your car keys to get my luggage," Father Wooster said cheerfully. "It's still in your back seat."

"Tony?"

Sullenly he reached in his pocket and drew out her keys, tossed them to the clergyman. But when he saw that Petrina was going to walk along out to the parking area, Tony accompanied them, preventing by his determined presence any private exchange.

After the bags had been transferred into the dusty improbable hulk of the pickup, Father Wooster climbed up into it and brought the motor to roaring activity, backed the truck around with an expert maneuver and sent it racketing down the road and out to the highway.

"Come along, Miss Marinta, and I'll get you settled upstairs," Petrina suggested. "Then we'll talk over what we can do about that kitchen."

Tony had never intended to allow her to remain at the house at all, she realized as they began to walk back across the yard. There never had been any choice as far as he was concerned—he had just let her think there was.

Barely concealed fury glittered in his eyes and stiffened his muscles with tension. He stalked around the house toward the back, leaving them to attend to Miss Marinta's bag and settling down by themselves.

Was this the man with whom she had thought she was in love only one short year ago, that she had been prepared to marry? She watched his retreating back, repelled.

Father Wooster's solution had caught Tony completely by surprise and it would take a while for him to get hold of himself. Though the presence of both Petrina and the clergyman's housekeeper was totally unacceptable to Tony, he had no idea what to do about it. Not yet.

That would change.

Petrina did not delude herself. Tony might be confused and angry at the moment but he would recover. Whatever he was up to was too important for him to sacrifice for what he could turn into a temporary setback. Since he obviously needed to be free from surveillance, he would have to try to rid himself of the burden of their proximity.

The two women were upstairs, Petrina settling the housekeeper into her bedroom, when they heard a car start up and saw Tony pull out of a protecting shed and take off down the lane without bothering to inform them either of where he was bound or of when he expected to return.

After Miss Marinta had investigated the contents of the refrigerator and freezer she announced, "We need a few things, Miss Gentry. Milk, butter, fruit, lettuce. There's a store in Cypress Glade ought to have some of it. You want to come in with me?"

"Will you be gone long?"

The black woman laughed. "There's not enough to choose from for me to stay long." She jerked her head toward the window. "He not be back before I am. He is a man with a lot on his mind. He has much driving to do before he calms down." She tucked her big handbag under her arm. "Better you should lie down here and rest for a while. You be safe."

"Then you take my car and attend to things. Here are the keys. And you'll need money." Petrina took several bills from her wallet and handed them to the housekeeper. "Let me know when you need more."

She had intended to unpack her own bags and hang up her clothes, once Miss Marinta was on her way. The hands on her watch read eleven forty-five—she could make an appointment to see Sam Brock later in the afternoon. He would still be in his office.

There had been a telephone extension upstairs in the hall alcove. She went out into the hallway and looked. It was still there but Linette had gotten a different instrument. This one was sleek and low-slung, the kind that would have numbered buttons instead of a dial, green against the cypress paneling of the alcove.

Miss Marinta was right. She did need a rest after the strain of the morning. Sam Brock could wait. She wanted to be alert and at her best when she talked to him, not tired and vulnerable and confused as she felt now. With a quick lithe motion she pulled her dress up over her head and laid it across a chair, keeping on her slip.

An hour, perhaps a little longer, had passed when she heard the housekeeper's big melodious voice float up from downstairs to announce her return. Petrina acknowledged the call without opening her eyes. She was dozing again when she heard a tap at the door.

"It's me, Marinta," the housekeeper said softly. "We better talk, Miss Gentry. I brought you some tea to wake you up."

"Come in." Petrina sat up. She felt sticky from sleeping in the humid warmth of early afternoon, but, once the sleep had been rubbed from her eyes, refreshed and far more capable of handling her problems. She sipped her tea and waited for the housekeeper to begin.

"That man, he was down in town talking with the lawyer over in his office. I saw the car parked out in front."

"Sam Brock is his lawyer," Petrina said mildly, glad that she had not called to make her appointment right then.

Miss Marinta's face showed no expression. "I heard some talk in town," she said. "I asked a lady there did anyone know why that man's wife run away. Did anyone know where she went."

Petrina swallowed hard. "You got right down to business, didn't you!"

Miss Marinta's eyelids dropped down over her eyes like black shades, raised slowly. "She say the whole town is talking and wondering what that man is going to do now. The oil people came and want to lease land your cousin owns, only her husband wants to handle all the business himself. Your cousin told some of the ladies all about that and said she wasn't going to turn over everything she owned to him even if they was married. Besides, there was more to it, only she was afraid to tell what she had found out."

It was like Linette to broadcast her affairs to her friends, Petrina thought.

Miss Marinta wasn't finished. "One lady said you were back here to get that man for yourself. Don't take long for news to get around this place, I tell you that. I said you don't want your cousin's man. She welcome to him, such as he is. You got one of your own."

"You think I have, do you?" Petrina's eyes glinted mischievously.

The big black woman got up and grinned down at her.

"Doesn't matter what I think. If it takes you having a man of your own to protect your reputation, that's what you get." She picked up the empty tea cup and started through the door.

"Thank you, Miss Marinta."

The housekeeper turned, her smile gentle. "Just Father Wooster calls me Miss Marinta," she said. "Everybody else call me Marinta and I'd like you to call me that too."

"All right," Petrina smiled back. "That will be nice."

She carried a change of clothes down to the big bathroom at the end of the hall, found towels in the linen cupboard where they used to be, and started to run a shower. For a little while, standing under the stinging spray, time seemed suspended in the simple pleasure of cool water on a warm day. She shampooed her hair under the shower and practiced her vocal exercises, the whole succession of vowel and consonant placements necessary to produce good clear speech without betraying lip movements. Finished, she mopped up the splashed water and spread her towels to dry, dusted herself with fragrant talc, splashed with cologne and dressed. She had laid out a plain yellow cotton print and slipped on white sandals. It didn't take long to get back into the habit of dressing to be comfortable in the subtropical climate of south Florida.

When she got back to her room she found Marinta unpacking suitcases and hanging away dresses and gowns. The housekeeper rolled her eyes in eloquent dismay.

"This closet wasn't made for all this finery," she said. "I got plenty of room left in the closet in my room. Would you like me to hang some of these costumes in there for you? I can keep a few of the suitcases in there for you, too. You try to keep them all in here and you won't have room to move!"

In the end, that's what they did, using the available

closet in Marinta's room for costume storage. Marinta ran her hand down the spangled English ball gown with evident pleasure. "These are mighty pretty dresses," she commented. "Someday maybe I can get to see you in one of your shows."

"Better than that, I'll give you a whole private one for yourself!" Petrina promised.

She got Peter up out of his case and sat him on the bed. Marinta picked up the Pedlar doll and stood looking it over with puzzled interest, trying to fit the tray in place, supported by the wide ribbon that went up around its neck.

"You have to put the ribbon in place first," Petrina said in Peter's most high officious voice. "Otherwise it won't work!"

Marinta jerked with surprise at the unexpected voice and the tray flew out of her hand, falling to the hardwood floor. "You scare a person to death talking like that," she scolded Peter, swung around to Petrina. "Wasn't him at all, was it? Wasn't that doll! You did the talking!" She looked down at the floor where several of the small objects had broken loose from the tray. "And look what I done to all the pretties! I'm sorry, Miss Gentry. I'm just not used to hearing something like him talk to me."

"It was my fault," Petrina laughed. "Don't worry about it. I'll just glue this stuff back on and everything will be fine."

Marinta fled and Petrina stooped down to gather together the scattered wares. She picked up a little pewter goblet and a tiny miniature doll that had broken loose, a silver thimble, and a painted ornament from a small velvet cap that was still attached to the tray. She was puzzled, looking at the cap. The ornament was grossly out of proportion for this cap and the cap itself did not seem to have been designed for the trimming. She looked at the bauble and saw that some of the paint had chipped off when it fell.

With her fingernail Petrina flicked off more scales of paint and her breath came shallow as she looked at what she held in her hand. The remaining paint prevented full refraction but it could not disguise the fact that she held a spectacular clear blue stone of very large size.

"Dear heaven!" she breathed. So this was why the Australian had been following her!

CHAPTER 14

For a few minutes Petrina held the collection of dis-
lodged Pedlar's wares in her palm, too shocked to think.
Then she heard the sound of an approaching car and
sprang to her feet. The wares had to be fastened back on
the tray—except for the painted stone—and she had to
find a substitute for that, to paste on its place, until she
was able to get in touch with David or Julian to find out
what action they wanted her to take. She had only to
safeguard the stone. It was Julian's job to deal with it.

Her heart pounded suffocatingly as she rummaged
through her repair kit looking for a tube of mending cement among the jumble of pliers and cutters and screw
drivers and various springs and cords she kept at hand in
case an emergency repair on Peter became necessary. At
last she found the tube and glued down the goblet, the
thimble, the miniature doll. A tiny dab of dried cement
clung to the small velvet cap. She flicked it off, tempted
to let it go without trying to find a substitute ornament to
glue on. But the velvet showed an imprint too obvious to
be ignored if anyone was looking.

Hands trembling, she dumped out the contents of her
case of costume jewelry, looking for a stone similar in size
to the painted one she held in her hand. Nothing there
would do. Despairing, she pushed it all back in the case.
She could drive into town but the chance of finding anything in a Cypress Glade store that could be substituted
for the bauble was practically zero.

Her English ball gown costume had a great many brilliants sewn here and there on it, though, and there were some fair-sized stones decorating the bodice. She dropped the painted stone into her pocket and went into Marinta's room to look at the dress. The stones on the skirt were much too small, but there were several on the bodice that were very close to the right size. Carefully she removed one from the neckline. It would show, but it could be replaced when she got back to Miami, where the dress had been made in the first place.

Tony was walking down the hall toward the big master bedroom overlooking the front of the house as she opened the door. She waited until he had passed, then dashed into her own room.

The original stone had been painted with dingy metallic silver. She had some silver nail enamel that was more shiny than the original but might pass. Holding the stone securely with a pair of tweezers, she painted it. It took two coats to cover the glass but when the enamel had dried there was little difference between the stones, even when they were close together.

She glued the substitute onto the Pedlar doll's tray and with shaking hands put it back in Peter's case for safekeeping as it dried, along with the doll itself.

All that remained was hiding the original safely. She looked at it. She could paint over it with the silver nail enamel, covering again the places where the paint had flicked off. That would disguise it once more but it still wouldn't hide it, not if a searcher knew what he was looking for and was determined to find it.

She sat down suddenly, stunned by the simplicity of a possible solution that flashed into her mind. She could simply remove the silver paint for the time being and glue the gem on the ball gown in place of the stone she had removed. The dress would not be used again for a while, and long before that she would have heard from Julian or American customs.

Pasting the blue stone in place took only a few seconds. Once in place it disappeared, lost in the midst of the dazzling glitter of the other stones. She thought of Tony crushing the body of the Pedlar doll, trying to feel the outline of some kind of contraband, while all along the secret had been openly displayed.

The Australian had said he would give her a week to think over making the exchange. Unless he had meant only to throw her off her guard, that would give her the time she needed. And if he did return sooner, there was nothing more to be done about it.

She went to the hall telephone and called Sam Brock's office. His secretary said that he was gone for the day but there was time available, that Petrina might have an hour late the next afternoon, and Petrina took it. So much accomplished.

The aroma of roast beef began to rise from the kitchen, mingled with other fragrances, vegetables, pastry with a fruit filling. She took a quick ecstatic breath. Father Wooster's loss of Marinta was most certainly a gain for this household.

There was one more call to be made. She got an overseas operator and gave her the number of David's hotel. The connection was made with little delay. It would be evening in London and telephone traffic would not be heavy. If David had left for the theater already she could leave a message for him. She listened incredulously to the operator, thanked her, stood staring blankly at the telephone before she finally returned it to its stand.

David had checked out of his hotel this morning and his forwarding address was confidential.

She could see Tony's door open slightly down the hall-way, a long sliver of late afternoon light bearing silent witness against the dark boards of the flooring. She wanted to place a call to Julian but the call would have to wait until later. There were things to ask and things to tell on which she could not have Tony eavesdrop.

Sitting at the small telephone shelf, looking toward the door opened only that thin amount which was necessary to permit sound to enter, she thought of Linette and how it might have been in those days, those hours, before she disappeared. Had she sat here frightened, wondering who she could call on for help? Had she dialed someone and caught sight of the door opening as her husband listened? And had she then given up, as Petrina was preparing to do now on her own call to Julian? Who might Linette have tried to telephone for help?

Petrina tried to picture Linette, who had wanted desperately so much of life and had been so incapable of standing on her own feet, talented only with an incredible fragile beauty that hadn't been quite enough to buy her passage out of this hated Everglades town in which she had grown up. She might have escaped with the money she inherited from Aunt Ellen but by then it was too late. Tony had discovered her.

Four days had passed since Linette had sent her cable to London. And she had been gone from this house, Sam Brock had told David, almost a week. It was getting on to two weeks, then, that Linette had been on her own, scavenging for food, shelter, whatever she needed. Perhaps even clothing, if she had fled the house abruptly.

Sick at heart and driven by a need to try to know more, if somehow she could manage it, Petrina wondered if she dared to step alone across the border of that meditative dimension to which David had introduced her only a few weeks ago, in London. He had taught her techniques, guided her—but this was very different. Here she was alone, vulnerable.

Petrina closed her eyes and slowly began to relax her muscles, turning her mind inward, reaching languorously down toward the dark quiet place inside her being.

Like a novice swimmer, apprehensively reaching for a floating bit of flotsam, she reached for a thought that drifted by and held it for a moment.

Back in London Catarina had psychometrized the Pedlar and Peter by reading the accumulated impressions left by people who had handled them. If surroundings or objects could absorb the emotions of humans driven by strong fear, of hate, of love, surely this spot at the telephone must have sponged up countless telltale impressions. She might not be able to accomplish what she had seen the Portuguese psychic do, but if she gleaned even a faint perception, it would be far more than she had yet done.

A flush of warm glimmering light touched the edges of her inner dark and worked slowly through, lightening and moving inward by slow degrees until a reassuring gentle radiance, clear and brilliant, lay across the receptive lining of her eyes.

Her breathing began to change and one at a time, she was conscious of changes in automatic functions, of a slower rush of blood through her veins and awareness of the difference, of a changed sensitivity of her skin as it reported air currents shifting, cool stirrings against the warm moist air, reported a change of light in the hallway behind her and a change in atmospheric heat as a large male figure drew closer, noiselessly.

"Hello, Tony," she murmured, her eyes still closed, insulated from him by her concentration.

"What the hell are you doing out here by the telephone?" he burst out angrily.

David had warned her that she must return from her inner reaches as slowly and methodically as she had entered them.

With great effort she kept herself from answering Tony. Slowly she began to release herself from her meditation and to turn outward again, carefully, holding herself away from the impact of this angry hostile man whose spirit was ravaged by the turmoil of his anxiety and greed. She could not do what David might have been able to do. She could not touch Tony's thoughts with her own and know them. And as she swayed, frightened by what she had done, she was glad.

He made no attempt to stop her when she moved away from him and went downstairs. Devils all his own consumed him as he went back into the big bedroom, slamming the door behind him. He did not reappear until Marinta sent a call for dinner caroling up the wide front stairway.

A blazing splash of sunset color painted the western sky by the time Marinta served dinner. Tony stared straight down at his plate and his silence was less sullen than totally preoccupied.

"I have an appointment with Sam Brock late tomorrow afternoon," Petrina told him.

He nodded without interest. "Why?"

"To see whether he can shed some light on Linette's disappearance."

A strange expression of sardonic amusement flickered across Tony's face and was gone. "It's possible," he said slowly. "Surely it is quite possible."

His slurred but careful speech made her wonder if he had been drinking during the two hours he spent up in his room. His face was slightly flushed and he patted away a thin film of perspiration. Overhead the big dining room fan kept its rhythmic broad blades moving the heavy air. From outside came a beginning chorus of tree frogs and a heavier answer returned from farther out in the saw grass, rosy briefly with reflected light.

"Does Sam know why Linette left?" Petrina asked blandly. "Do you, Tony?"

She was thinking of the conversation Marinta had reported hearing in town and her hazel eyes examined his face feature by feature as though she had never really had it in focus before. She watched his gray eyes go to the windows, to the bureau against the wall, everywhere but to her face.

"If I knew where she was, I'd have her back here," Tony answered. "I don't know why she left. I thought she was happy here. Maybe she was depressed about something."

"Why are there search parties in the Glades?" Petrina pursued. "What was it that made people think she might have gotten lost out there?"

"She took that airboat your aunt used to keep down on the slough. It was found abandoned near one of the canals and Ira identified it and had it hauled back here."

He didn't know about the cable Linette had sent from Miami. Fortunately Tony was occupied with serving himself another portion of Marinta's elegantly roasted beef so he missed any betraying hint of expression that might have crossed her face.

The telephone rang back in the downstairs study and Tony got up automatically to attend to it, halted as it was answered mid-ring by Marinta. He remained standing, expecting to be called and told—what?

Petrina watched his handsome features compose themselves in expectation. But Marinta was looking toward Petrina when she came to the dining room door.

"For you, Miss Gentry."

The study was on the opposite side of the house from

the dining room, out of earshot, but Petrina closed the door anyhow. She held the telephone in her hand for a second before she could trust her voice.

The sound of David's "Hello, love" reached out to her.

"Where have you been?" Her voice raveled away before she had quite finished.

David laughed softly. "Busy, love. Very very busy." The line crackled ominously and he continued hurriedly. "I had a chance to take a brief leave from the theater and I grabbed it. Nora was able to get me a ticket with the same airline you took and I got in this afternoon at Miami."

Petrina heard a faint sound and the volume of David's voice was slightly reduced. Had Tony gone to the upstairs telephone to listen?

"Do you have an extra bedroom you might let me use?" David continued smoothly, though he must have been aware of the change in telephone transmission, too. "Impetuously, I took off across the state to be with you and I discover now that I am in Cypress Glade that there is no hotel."

"Of course, David. We have five bedrooms here—lots of room." She held the phone between her hands as though it had a treasured life of its own. "Where are you calling from?"

He chuckled. "A filling station cum variety counter cum fishing tackle store. There are other things here. I don't see an identification sign anywhere, though."

"I know where you are. Ask the man who runs it to direct you to the house. Everyone in Cypress Glade knows where it is. You can't get lost."

"I'll see you soon." He rang off.

When she returned to the dining room she found Tony there, his gray eyes malevolent and probing. It would have been a substantial breathless race for him to have gotten to the dining room from upstairs, past Marinta, and he was not breathing hard. Perhaps she had been mistaken about the telephone.

"A friend of mine finds himself in Cypress Glade. I invited him to stay here, if you have no objection." She sipped her coffee, watching him closely.

He cut himself a bite of beef, put it in his mouth, chewed it, his eyes focused on the deepening red glare of the sinking sun through the bank of windows to his right. When he looked back at her there was no anger, no hostility in his gray eyes. There was something far more frightening. There was no emotion at all. His eyes were still and icy cold as death itself as his lips moved in a meaningless smile.

"Of course we can put him up, Petrina," he said. "No problem. We have plenty of room." The slur was gone from his voice.

CHAPTER 15

Petrina had wondered many times over during the past year what it would be like when David and Tony finally met. It had never occurred to her to doubt that they would meet. Fatalistically, it was "when" in her mind, not "if" when she thought about it. And, as if to prepare herself, she had tried to imagine how it would happen and when. Probably before or after a performance somewhere, she would think, or at a restaurant. Perhaps at an airport. Absolutely unexpectedly David and she would encounter Tony and Linette in some busy public place. Never in any projection had it occurred to her that the meeting might take place here in the shelter of this brooding old house at Cypress Glade.

She could not sit at the table any longer with Tony's implacable gray eyes watching her like shining metallic disks.

"I'm going outside to wait for him," she said.

"There is some mosquito repellent in the spray can on the console out in the hall," he replied absently. "You'll need it if you are outside for long."

"I remember. The mosquitoes come in clouds. Aunt Ellen used to keep spray out there, too." He made no offer to join her as she left the room and she was glad.

A warm night breeze touched her face as she looked off into the thicket that lined the lane and she felt her pulse quicken as she caught sight of the first glow of David's headlights. The swift subtropical dark was bringing down a quick curtain to what little was left of the flaming sunset glow.

The car moved rapidly up the road, lights on high beam until a turn in direction brought them focused full on her as she stood on the veranda, waiting. For a second they picked her out, rested on her, then fell to low in a protective reaction that was a strangely intimate extension of David himself.

She stepped off the veranda and down on the packed sand. The car pulled up to the side, stopped and suddenly the lights were turned off entirely. The car door opened and David stepped out into the heavy dusk and looked down at her and without a word held out his arms in greeting and gathered her close. His face, as he stood in the shadows, had the chiseled planed beauty of a dark carved mask.

"I missed you, Trina," he told her, his voice rough. The light kiss that began as part of hello changed as his mouth touched hers. His arms suddenly tightened hard and his lips moved against hers in an unmistakable message of need and passion. Instinctively she responded to the heat that flared through him and the happiness she felt at having him there.

"I missed you, too," she whispered, her lips parted to his, her body molded against him.

The screen door opened with a sharp click in the stillness. "Would you like a hand with your bags?" Tony called out.

The pressure of David's arms relaxed and Petrina stepped away.

"Thank you. I can manage nicely," David replied without inflection.

Tony had interrupted them deliberately, Petrina was very sure. He stood holding the door open as David carried in two suitcases. Once they gained the lighted hallway both David and Tony stopped and surveyed each other coolly as Petrina introduced them to one another.

"So you are Tony Addison," David said evenly. "I've heard quite a bit about you."

The muscles of Tony's mouth moved irritably. "You have the advantage there," he returned. "I haven't heard anything about you."

"You wouldn't have." David picked up the bags he had put down when they were introduced. "I met Petrina after you had married her cousin. Petrina told me about your wife's disappearance. Has there been any news of her yet?"

"None." Tony's face was rigidly under control but his hand, as he lighted a cigarette, trembled slightly. "We keep hoping and searching but we haven't found a sign of her. She seems to have gone from the face of the earth."

"Surely not. There will be word of her soon, I'm sure." David's dark eyes were intent. "Trina, perhaps you will show me to whatever room you have assigned me and I'll get this luggage out of the way. We'll be back down to join you shortly, Tony."

He motioned Petrina to precede him up the wide stairway and she began to climb, aware that something oddly like the first stylized movements of a fencing exhibition had taken place between the two men. There had been the salute, the on guard, then the thrust and parry. And there would surely be more to complete the sequence for them before they were finished with each other.

Petrina led David down the hall, explaining the plan of the upstairs as she went. "The master bedroom overlooks the front of the house," she told him. "This is the room Marinta is using. She is our acting housekeeper right now. My room is next to hers. I'm putting you across the hallway from us. If you're up early you can watch the sun rise."

"Heaven forbid." He followed her inside his room and put his suitcases on the bed. "This is the first time we will be sharing the same roof, Trina. It's a very pleasant feeling." His dark eyes gently ran over her face, stilled when they reached her lips, and then decisively he turned away.

He walked about the room, examining the heavy Victorian dresser with its mirror that was tarnished near the framing wood, the big high bed bracketed head and foot with more carved Victorian wood. "This is a nice old house," he said slowly. "It's much larger than I had thought."

"There are the five bedrooms up here," she told him. "And the usual rooms downstairs. Downstairs two parlors, formal and family, face each other across the hall. Then on the west side the dining room and across the hall on the east side, the study. The kitchen and pantries and a small breakfast room that isn't used anymore are at the back of the house, and a storeroom. There's the big stairway you came up at the front of the house and another one from the second floor to a kitchen pantry in back. One telephone is in the study, and the other is on the second floor."

David halted his prowling and looked at her in surprise. "I would have guessed there were three telephones," he said reflectively. "Another one downstairs, in the kitchen perhaps. Or possibly in one of the parlors. Are you sure there are only two, Trina?"

She told him about the feeling she'd had when he called that Tony might have been listening on another telephone, and hurriedly, softly, she rushed through an account of what had happened since she had arrived. David listened silently, interrupting her only once when

he went to the door and glanced up and down the hallway, then closed the door and drew her over to the far
side of the room to finish her story.

There was a worn hospitable linen upholstered wing
chair near the wide window. David sat down and leaned
back, his eyes shuttered for a few minutes after she had
finished.

"I must let Julian know what has happened," he said,
finally. "And where he can reach me. And I must call Catarina. She will be in Atlanta for the next week leading a
seminar on metaphysics. She can come if we need her."

"If we need her?" Petrina's mind flew back to that
spine-chilling reading Catarina had give Morag O Cathan
in London. "David, is Morag here? Is that what you
mean?"

His eyes opened, dark and intent, fixed on the changing faint light and pink-lined shadow reflected on the
water visible between the tall waving sea of grass that
stretched off in a black twilight wash toward the horizon.
"I wasn't thinking of Morag, Trina. Would you show me
to the telephone—I'll put in the calls and come downstairs
and join you."

She led him out to the alcove and realized he wanted
her to go downstairs to ensure privacy from another possible intrusion.

Heels clicking against the uncarpeted portion of the
upstairs hall she hurried along. Tony had just emerged
from the study, drink in hand, when she reached the bottom of the staircase. "David has a couple of calls to make.
He'll be along directly." She'd spoiled Tony's plans, judging by his sullen resentment. They walked on to the family west living room together.

"I'll fix you a drink." He dropped ice in her glass,
splashed in a measure of bourbon, added a little water.
"May as well make one for David at the same time." He

built another, giving the job much more time and concentration than it warranted. Even so, he had finished and David still had not returned. He paced nervously up and down the room a couple of times and finally he sat down, facing her. "So you met him in Miami, did you? What does he do?"

Petrina looked at the handsome petulant face with distaste. "I'm not quite sure I understand what you mean, Tony. Do you mean how does he make a living?" She sipped her drink slowly, her eyes fixed unwaveringly on him. Her back was to the hall door so she did not see David approach.

"I'm a mentalist." David's voice was pleasant, detached as he answered for himself.

"What the hell is a mentalist exactly?" Tony asked lightly. "Some sort of magician? A mind reader?"

David smiled. "Actually I began as a magician. A mentalist is a little of all of it, I suppose. And something else entirely. For instance, I just used a telephone upstairs—I asked the operator for charges, incidentally, and I left a check for the amount on the table up there. While I was using that telephone I followed the direction of the electrical flow of the telephone wire in this house—it's a process a little like dowsing—and I came to an interesting conclusion. There is also a telephone in the study. And there are two telephone jacks without phones plugged into them at this moment. One is in the kitchen. The other is in this room, out of sight behind that bar. The third telephone, which can be plugged into either jack as desired, is on the windowsill, hidden behind the draperies. Am I correct?"

The color had drained from Tony's face leaving it pallid beneath his careful tan. "That's quite a performance. Are your talents confined to following wires?"

David shrugged. "No. I told you, I do a little of all

sorts of things. Would you like me to tell you the number on that twenty-dollar bill in your wallet?" Without waiting for the other man's consent, David said deliberately, "G 51918051 D. You might check it."

Tony pulled his wallet from his pocket and his shocked expression as he removed a bill and read its number was all the verification needed.

"I do my particular thing at theaters mostly, sometimes nightclubs," David continued. "Lots of times on TV, both my own shows and guest shots. I also instruct parapsychology courses at a couple of universities when I am invited and able to accept. Is that drink for me, Addison?" He took the drink waiting on its coaster at the corner of the bar. "Thank you."

The clink of ice as he raised his glass to drink was oddly muted by the soft whup of the moving fan overhead.

"May I ask what business you are in?" David's tone was of polite interest, no more, but Tony's eyes narrowed.

"I'm into investment counseling." He walked over to the bar to replenish his empty glass. "I do some real estate work, too." His stiff back challenged David to probe further.

"It must be difficult to conduct your affairs from a location like this," David said mildly. He turned his head, as though he heard something on the softly stirring breeze outside the window. "You are going to have a visitor very soon. Someone quite old, I would say."

Tony's skin remained a muddy gray tone as he stared out of the front window across the veranda, dimly luminous with diffused light from the house, and out into the deepening black of the area beyond. He said nothing as they waited.

After about ten minutes the first faint sound of a laboring ancient pickup came drifting on the heavy moist night air. The sound grew louder, multiplied as though an old truck were pulling an equally old and heavy load on a trailer. At last they saw light flickering behind wind-stirred brush as the chorus of night insects changed in tone and volume.

The pickup thundered up the road and dexterously swept around so that it was pointing back down the road when it came to a stop, its trailer snugly positioned behind it. On the trailer reared an airboat scarred by years of battling the wiry abrasive stretches of saw grass in the Glades. The boat itself was like a flat-bottomed skiff. Even in the dim diffused light from the windows of the house, the shapes of the two high chairs, one behind another, were visible. And towering airily behind the chairs rose the wire-caged motor that drove a great propeller.

They stood waiting at the front door while a bent but agile lean figure jumped down from the pickup's cab.

"Ira!" Petrina shrieked, in recognition. She ran out and threw her arms around the old man, who wrapped her in a vigorous hug of his own. He had helped her past some very hard times in the old days, when she had first come here, sometimes just by listening patiently as she talked things through.

"I heard you were back here and I wanted to see for myself. I'm not coming in, thanks," as she threw open the door for him. "We put in a hard day today looking and I'm bushed. I wanted to tell you, you can come with me tomorrow for a while. There's an Airboat Association dock off the trail south of here, you know where it is, and if you're there about two o'clock tomorrow I'll pick you up. No objection if you want to bring your company."

"I'll be there," she agreed immediately. "You, David?"

"Count on it."

Even though Tony was standing outlined in the doorway by the hallway light, Ira ignored him as though he did not exist.

"I'm glad you're back here, Miss Gentry," Ira said. "Don't you worry. We'll find Miss Linette. You'll see. She knows the Glades."

They watched him go back to his truck and send it briskly out into the waiting darkness.

David yawned, apologized for it as they went back into the house. "I think I'll go up and turn in," he told them. "We'll have a big day ahead tomorrow."

"I'll go up with you." Petrina turned to Tony. "Good night, Tony. See you in the morning."

He turned away without answering.

As David had said, it was very pleasant being together under one roof. He bent and kissed her forehead as they paused before their doors. "I plan on going to Miami tomorrow early," he said. "Would you like to come along? Leaving about eight? We'll easily be able to make it back in time to meet Ira at the dock."

"I'd love to. Anything special?"

"Very special." Briefly he held her close. "I telephoned Catarina while I was upstairs and asked her to fly to Miami tomorrow. I also took the liberty of inviting her to stay here for the weekend, if she's able to arrange it. I think you might be glad to have her."

"I hope she can do it! Did you reach Julian?"

"I talked to him. Several months ago there was talk that a stone had surfaced on the continent and had been taken to England—it might have been one of the fabled remnant stones of the Hope diamond. A dealer in London was holding the stone for appraisal and sale to a syndicate when it was stolen in a modus operandi that fitted the other terrorist thefts. If the stone you have is that stone, it should not be hard to recognize it. The Hope blue is the darkest sapphire-blue diamond in existence."

"The dress is in Marinta's closet. You could look at the stone yourself."

"Too late in the evening now, and we don't want to draw attention to it, anyhow. Julian is having an expert sent from New York to look it over and their man will be working with the United States Customs people. They will have their best men on the job to protect this stone and to catch Tyron, you can be sure of that. They've been after him for a long time."

"Do you think Tyron will wait a week before he comes back?"

David regarded her soberly. "No more than you do. You have to think that if it is one of the missing Hope remnants, its value is almost impossible to calculate. It would depend on what a collector would be willing to pay. The color is truly unique. There was originally a huge blue Indian brilliant of sixty-seven carats stolen at the time of the French Revolution. That gem was never recovered. Some experts believe the Hope diamond, which is of this color, was cut from that stone. You can be sure that if the stone you have is a remnant, Tyron will be moving heaven and earth to get it back. The terrorists would be able to buy a whole arsenal for what that stone would bring."

"Can't we take the stone into Miami and turn it over to someone there?"

"It's a long drive to Miami, Trina, and too many things could happen to us on the way, things that we're not prepared to cope with. This is a police matter. I just wish you had never been involved at all."

They heard Tony's step on the stairs.

"I'll call you early," David promised. "Night, love!"

Once inside her room, Petrina turned the big key in the lock, then pulled one of the heavy mahogany side chairs over to the door and hooked it under the knob. She might not be able to keep a dedicated prowler out of her room while she was away from it, and she was resigned to that. But she was not about to be invaded while she was asleep.

CHAPTER 16

Promptly at seven a stealthy knock on her door and David's voice growling softly, "Up, you lazy thing! Up!" brought Trina wide awake.

She raced to the door and cautioned, "Hush! Do you want to wake everybody? I'm up!"

Awkward and half awake she fumbled with the chair and finally got it pulled away from the door knob, turned the big key. Long since David's door had closed, probably behind him as he went down to the kitchen. A murmur of voices came up the back stairwell as she hurried to the bathroom with her bundle of towels and clothing, soap and cosmetics.

An imposing breakfast was spread on a plank table at the windowed side of the large kitchen. Marinta had cooked sausages, scrambled eggs, made hotcakes—even laid out dishes of strawberries, in at the market from Plant City up near Tampa. David was sitting in the morning sunshine, his saturnine face more relaxed than she had ever seen it, his eyes watching the door for her even as he exchanged pleasantries with Marinta, busy still at the kitchen range.

Marinta started to lay out a bountiful quantity of food on Petrina's plate, then shook her head. "You didn't get that figure working your way through the kind of breakfast I put together."

"I'm pretty good with breakfast," Petrina corrected. "It's later on that I go short. But I don't usually eat at this hour, either. I am not usually up at this hour, matter of fact." But Marinta's feather-light hotcakes with the jug of hot syrup beside them made too enticing a combination to resist. "More coffee," she requested, "and more sausage, please." She hadn't had that pistol-hot southern-style sausage since the last breakfast she had eaten in this house after Aunt Ellen's funeral. For a moment the sausage taste was sawdust and the swallowing difficult.

David's hand came down over hers briefly and she wondered if he guessed what had passed through her thoughts.

"Did you ever see anything that wispy eat that formidably much?" he asked Marinta.

"Man that marries her has to be ready to breakfast an elephant!" she whooped.

"Good grief!" Petrina pushed her plate away and got up, reconsidered and speared one more bit of sausage while the two watchers laughed uproariously. "Who ever heard of feeling that cheerful in the morning?"

"I like a man feels good in the morning," Marinta approved. "Never did think much of one come grouching around and nobody even waked up yet."

"You see?" David drank the rest of his coffee and led the way out through the house to his car in front.

It was the first time she had really looked at the car he had rented. Big and powerful, the white automobile he had chosen was capable of pulling itself through rugged terrain, just as it was designed to outrun most machines not in its class.

"You could drag almost anyone with this beauty," Petrina admired.

"Let's hope I don't have to," David returned, seriously.

He settled her down beside him and turned on the ignition. The big car turned over and growled softly as it warmed up. He turned on the windshield wipers and while they were clearing a pattern in the heavy morning dew, jumped out and rubbed away the moisture from the other windows with a handful of paper towels.

A faint motion behind the upstairs window overlooking the veranda caught her attention. She glanced up, suddenly aware that Tony was watching from the master bedroom. He knew that they were meeting Ira at two and he knew of her appointment with the lawyer late in the afternoon. But it must have been puzzling and irritating to have them take off at this hour. Marinta knew only that they were gone for the day, so she would have been able to give him no answers if he inquired of her later.

David drove swiftly along the approach roads and soon they were up on Alligator Alley, speeding along headed east. He reached into his pocket and pulled out a pair of dark glasses, put them on, swung down the sun visor.

As he drove, he checked the rear-vision mirror regularly. She started to turn around to look back down the road once she noticed his action and he said crisply, "Keep your attention straight ahead, Trina!"

He dropped the car's speed by ten miles an hour. Two cars passed them but she could see by his expression that he was still waiting for something else to happen. Finally he brought the car's speed back up to what it had been.

"We've been followed ever since we left the county road and got up on the Alley," he said. "A green sedan has been staying back far enough so I haven't been able to see the driver's features clearly, but it has stayed the same distance back regardless of how I've varied my own speed. We're being followed, all right. And I'm pretty sure the driver is a man, middle-aged and heavy." He smiled. "No beard. Baldish."

"And you don't want me to turn around and see if I might recognize him?"

David nodded consent. "It can't matter now, I suppose.

If he'd intended any harm he'd have stopped us back on that deserted stretch. Or tried to." David patted the dashboard. "He'd have had his work cut out for him."

Petrina unfastened her seat belt and twisted around, held her position draped over the back of her seat as she pretended to be reaching for something in the rear of the automobile. She had seen that dust-stained late-model sedan before, when she was driving through Cypress Glade with Father Wooster on her way to the house yesterday. It had been pulled up near the filling station, poorly parked so it had blocked enough of the narrow road to necessitate her slowing down and carefully easing around it. The filling station was only a few doors from Sam Brock's office.

Frowning as she chased an elusive memory, she finally pinned it down. "I've seen him before. I think he has a little insurance agency with desk space in Sam Brock's building. He did some jobs for Brock, too, legwork things, chasing down information. Nothing like a real investigator." She waved her hands outward to the miles of empty swampland. "It doesn't take much looking to find out everybody's secrets around here."

"I don't know about that," David said slowly. "Linette's absence hasn't been all that easy to figure out."

Petrina settled back again, thinking about the car in back. "I don't even remember his name. I hardly knew him. He'd have no reason to be following me—unless Brock sent him. Unless Brock saw us drive through town and wondered what we were up to." She shook her head. "Brock would have no reason to be interested in our business. Besides, I have an appointment with him at four this afternoon. He could ask me whatever he wanted to know then."

"Would you really tell him anything?" David threw back his head and laughed with genuine amusement.

"I'm sure that Sam Brock is well aware that anything he wants to know about your affairs he'll have to find out for himself." He drove for a while in silence. "It does bring up an interesting point, though. I wonder what exactly Sam Brock could be concerned about. Do you suppose he's partnered in something with Tony and that the two of them have something directly to do with Linette's disappearance?"

"They do want to find her."

"I'm sure of that, too." David slapped the steering wheel impatiently. "They must have good reason. I can understand why the woman's husband would want to know where she is, if for no other reason than that oil deal. What I don't understand is why Sam Brock would send someone to follow us. What is *his* interest in us or her that makes him think you might know where she is?"

"Maybe he thinks she told us more than she did when she sent the cable."

"That's possible. It's logical." He glanced sidelong at her. "Buckle your damn seat belt!"

She shrugged and buckled, untroubled by his manner. He was not signaling some automotive manuever that would require that she be secured by the belt. He had simply used her omission as a way to let off steam. Behind them the green car kept its distance and ahead lay the blank ribbon of road stretching across the Everglades. Rippling stands of saw grass stretched off toward the horizons on either side, dotted with infrequent islands of trees.

"There are poison manchineel trees out there," she told him softly. "They're tall and beautiful and the flowers are pretty and fragrant and later there is fruit that has a wonderful aroma. And all of it is poisonous—the fruit, the sap, the leaves. Even the rain or dew that drips from its leaves will poison someone sheltering under it. But Linette knows the manchineel. She wouldn't mistake it for something else."

David let her talk without commenting.

"And there are strangler figs and poisonwood. Poisonwood is beautiful, too. It looks like gumbo limbo and it glistens in the sunlight. Any part of it can burn and blister. I was in the hospital for a week, once, after I tried to gather sap for Ira's wife. She makes medicine of it that she uses as an emetic, sudorific, sedative—she has even treated rheumatism and other disorders with it."

She shivered, looking out over the saw grass. "The grass doesn't look as high as it is, David. It grows six and eight feet high out there and it cuts like broken bottles. If you should step out into it you could sink down in the muck and fall and you couldn't use the grass to help pull yourself up again because it would cut your hands to ribbons. There's a special bacteria native to the Glades that causes horrible virulent infections to wounds, David."

"That's enough," he stopped her crisply. "If she is out there, she knows how to cope with the dangers a lot better than you or I. You won't do her any good at all tolling off horrors like a chain of black beads."

Her eyes were blurred with tears as she turned to him. "With you here beside me I can actually say what I know is out there," she said softly. "Before I couldn't. Do you think she's still alive, David?"

He kept his eyes straight ahead, the lines of his thin face impassive. "Yes."

"Will we find her? Soon enough?"

This time he hesitated before he answered. "Yes."

She sat back and closed her eyes. "Will Catarina stay out at the house with us over the weekend? We could bring her back to the airport anytime she wanted so she could return to Atlanta and her seminar."

"I think she will stay with us," David said.

"You and Catarina are old friends, aren't you?"

"We go back many years together, yes."

She sensed that he did not want to talk more about Catarina and yet she could not let the subject be. "You knew Morag O Cathan before, too, didn't you?"

The lines of David's face tightened bleakly. "Yes, I did. A long time ago."

An alien chill seemed to touch her and she shivered. There was something here that he did not want to discuss with her but that he would not conceal if she asked him about it. She wasn't sure that she wanted to ask the questions that would unlock an answer. She was remembering the reading Catarina gave Morag and the part David took in the proceedings. There was so much she didn't know about David. But there were important things she did know. She knew his kindness, his generosity, his integrity, his goodness.

David's lips curved with grim amusement. "No more questions?" When she didn't answer, the smile softened suddenly. "Someday I will probably tell you a good many things you may in the end find you would rather not know. But not now."

They spoke very little during the rest of the ride but the silence was curiously companionable, as though they had come to some kind of turning point and had made a kind of pact.

"Keep an eye out for Catarina," David said, as they approached the sprawling buildings that curved to house the business of Miami International Airport.

There was no sign of Catarina's easily identified back-clad sturdy figure balanced and supported by her dark carved cane. Behind them, as David eased slowly along, trailed the green car, closer this time, as though determined not to lose them in traffic. Finally David parked and went inside the terminal. Petrina watched the green car move into another space nearby, then she turned away and ignored it.

When David returned he had Catarina with him and he carried a worn black valise. With deference and ceremony he stowed the elderly woman in the back seat and the black valise in the trunk. They exchanged a few words of greeting in Portuguese, switched to English.

"Are you doing well with your students?" David asked her.

Her mouth puckered eloquently. "There are very few serious students." Her black eyes rested on Petrina and the contact was almost physical. "And you, David tells on the telephone that you in your innocence have made the discovery for Julian of the stolen gem."

"Not innocence," Petrina corrected. "Accident."

"*Sim*," Catarina nodded. "It was most certainly accident."

Petrina wasn't sure whether it was the necessity to concentrate on her words because of the accent, or whether it was the tone itself, but she felt more was meant than said.

As though in confirmation Catarina put her hand on David's shoulder. "You asked me on the telephone could I stay with you this weekend. I stay, David."

"I'm glad. Now, where do you ladies choose to eat?"

"How about that fine seafood place out on Biscayne Boulevard? Do you like seafood, Catarina?" Petrina waited.

"As long as it is *bacalhau*," Catarina returned and laughed heartily.

"More like bouillabaisse, at the place Petrina means," David grinned. "The Portuguese relish for cod—*bacalhau*—has to be encountered to be believed, Trina. Say 'fish' to Catarina and there is only one, the faithful friend, the cod."

Catarina responded to his teasing with a wave of her hand in dismissal. "We have an hour before a civilized restaurant will serve us. Let us drive and see what changes in this city," she suggested grandly.

"Anywhere you would like to go, Trina?" David asked.

"Not especially." She thought. "You've seen the place at Cypress Glade. Would you like to see the house Aunt Ellen owned here in Miami? It's in the old section. As I told you, Aunt Ellen used to rent it out after my uncle died and I went in with her once to inspect the place when she was going to hire a contractor to do repairs. I don't know whether Linette still owns the property or not, or whether it was sold after Aunt Ellen died."

"We see," Catarina said firmly, not waiting for David to answer.

"Is that green car still behind us or has he given up now that we picked up Catarina?" David asked. "I can't see him in the rear vision."

"He's still there. Three cars back. There's a van and a bug and a sports car and then him."

David laughed. "He's going to have some fascinating morning sight-seeing!"

With Petrina directing, they drove down Flagler Street and entered "Little Havana" with its colorful stores and bursts of Spanish melody surging from one or another of the tobacco shops, bars, bookstores and open-front cafés lining the streets. It had been a year since Petrina had seen these streets, and even in that length of time, the change was apparent. The Cubans had revitalized the area and made it their own prosperous section.

They drove on farther with Petrina continuing to direct until they moved along a very secluded narrow street with little traffic. The green car stayed doggedly behind although the driver's face, even at his distance behind, was weary and shiny, stolid with the boredom of his task.

"Evidently he has been told to follow us and he has no choice," David said. "I don't intend to make it any more exciting for him by trying to lose him, either. Wait until he sits in the sun waiting for us to finish our lunch. He'd hardly dare to—"

Petrina stiffened. "David, that blond girl across the street up near the end of the block—she looks like Linette—"

Catarina levered herself up and Petrina felt strong fingers bite into her shoulders. "*Por Deus do ceu!*" Catarina gasped. "If you value the life of that poor creature do not turn your head toward her. Do not show that you recognize her! I see danger around her!"

Petrina obeyed, but rebelliously. "Aunt Ellen's house is just two blocks from here," she said. "If that is Linette, she may have been hiding there. We can go to the house and wait for her—" Her heart was pounding with the need to do something, to take action. "David, stop the car and let me get out."

"No." David eased the car past a large moving van and stopped for a signal light at the end of the block. "You cannot chance frightening her into flight. You can't draw attention to her unless you're prepared to turn her over to Tony and Brock immediately."

For just a few seconds the blond girl's eyes met Petrina's with absolutely no trace of recognition. Linette's blue eyes were wide and unfocused, numbed to anything that was going on around her.

"David, it is Linette," Petrina breathed. "She didn't know me. My God, what has happened to her?"

"That is why you must not show you know her," Catarina said. "We must not come back for her until later, when it is safe."

Linette turned the corner, walked across the lawn of a big two-story house, which appeared to be vacant. There was a battered for-sale sign leaning at an angle on the sparsely grassed area near the front door. The blond girl did not walk up the front steps. Instead she made her way around the side of the house toward the back.

The stop light changed and David sent his big car forward, straight ahead. The green car with its heavy-faced bored driver followed behind. Petrina took a deep breath and sank limply back against the seat, weak with relief as she saw that the man did not even glance toward the big house near the corner.

CHAPTER 17

The planned luncheon became as much a needed release from tension as it was a physical replenishment. They arrived at the Sea Gate restaurant before twelve, early enough so they were seated immediately and welcomed personally by the owner, an old friend of David's. Their order was simple: bouillabaisse, a light chef's salad, a great basket of hot hard-crusted breads with a big bowl of butter chips.

Catarina surveyed her tureen of fish chowder critically, pleasurably. "Eel," she identified. "Clam, shrimp, lobster." She tasted. "Snapper, flounder—"

"Enough!" David demurred. "We must be out of here within an hour. Petrina has an appointment to meet with her friend at an airboat dock on the Tamiami Trail at two o'clock. Let us agree that there are at least the required eight different kinds of fish and that there is also the necessary eel, which is fresh and very good. The chowder here is famous, Catarina. My friend owns a fishing boat which supplies him with fresh fish for his restaurant."

She pinned him with her black eyes. "Did you know that in parts of Europe it is believed being rubbed with the fat of eel makes you see fairies?"

"Yes? And did you know that it is also believed that dropping a live eel in the drink of a drunkard will cure him of the bad habit?"

"I concede the contest." She burst into laughter. "This bouillabaisse is *muito bem*. It is truly fine."

Petrina was halfway through her bowl of chowder when a question occurred to her. "No doubt the sight of a live eel swimming in a glass of anything would be enough to reform a drunkard. But will eel oil really make you see fairies or a facsimile, Catarina?"

Catarina broke off a crust of hot roll. "How would I know such a thing?" she countered blandly. "You think I am an old *bruxa*, that I might oil myself with eels to find this out, eh?"

David glanced at his watch. "Time to leave, I'm afraid."

The brief respite from the problem of helping Linette without exposing her to more danger was ended. They emerged from the cool dimly lighted restaurant into the hot muggy light of the parking lot. The green car, its driver's face flushed and sullen from the heat of waiting, was pulled up against a wall at the far side of the lot. When David's heavy car pulled out into the traffic of Biscayne Boulevard, the green car moved swiftly to follow.

David drove south until he reached the Tamiami Trail, then headed west along the older of the two paved roads that crossed the Everglades east to west. The Trail was only two lanes wide and after they had left the city behind, Petrina was very conscious of the deep canal alongside and the green car that kept close behind.

She tried to relax as the miles sped by but her mind kept returning to Linette. In the back seat Catarina dozed fitfully.

"Once I get you both back to the house, I will return to Miami alone and do what I can," David offered. "But they will be watching you. You can't do anything other than what you are doing."

"There is no point in my going out with Ira, now. We know Linette isn't out there," Petrina said. "I expect he and Sara will be very happy that Linette has been located. Ira can get back about his own business now, too."

"They both are very fond of Linette, aren't they?" David asked.

Tears stung her eyes unexpectedly. "They loved Linette. They were here with Aunt Ellen even before Linette came, were with Aunt Ellen and Uncle E.Z. when they had both the Miami place and the one in Cypress Glade. After Uncle E.Z. died, they lived out here with Aunt Ellen and Linette. They were very kind to me, too, David. When I first came to Cypress Glade I hurt from the inside of my bones all the way out to my skin. I missed my father and our old life, and living out at the big house was like having been sent to another planet. Ira and Sara were good and loving."

"Do you trust Ira, then, and his wife?" David asked.

"Implicitly. With my life, if I had to."

"With Linette's life and safety, possibly?" His words had a sharp bite.

She sat stiffly, staring out at the willow-bordered canal and the saw grass beyond it, feeling the slow thump of her heart as she thought of what David might be suggesting.

"We could stop and talk to Ira. He could go to Miami and get Linette and no one would bother him at all. He could bring her back to Sara and Sara could care for her. Surely there must be some doctor we could call who wouldn't feel obliged to report to Tony or turn her over to him."

David said nothing in reply and she looked hopelessly at the set line of his chin.

She asked despairingly, "There aren't many options, are there? He is her husband and he has his legal rights."

"Didn't you say that Sara was a healer?" David questioned her. "The one who had you gathering poison-wood?"

She was surprised to have him remember so exactly. "I suppose you could say that. She gathers herbs, curative things. Peppergrass pods for liver trouble, snakebark for dysentery, bird pepper as an antidote for poisoned fish, ilex cassine for a purge or emetic. The 'black drink' of some Seminole Indian ceremonies is brewed from ilex cassine. People come to her from all over the state, David. She used to have hundreds of jars of different things and knew what everything was and what it did. Branches and leaves were always hanging around the kitchen drying." She took a deep breath. "Yes, I think that Sara could care for her."

The airboat docking compound sprawled ahead and David began to slow down, the automobile behind him following suit.

"Surely he won't stop here, too," Petrina sighed deject-edly. "How can we talk to Ira with him prowling around trying to eavesdrop?"

"I help," Catarina promised from the back seat. "You see. He will be no trouble."

Ira stood near the dock, waiting for them. His brown sun-baked face creased with displeased surprise at the green car pulling up alongside them and at the heavy-set man who stepped out of it and into the afternoon heat. Petrina moved swiftly toward the airboat, tethered to the dock, and Ira followed her out onto the dock, his eyes bright with surmise.

"Buck been tailing you?" he demanded.

She nodded. "Ira, we saw Linette in Miami, about a block from Aunt Ellen's old house. The house looked empty and there was a for-sale sign on the lawn. We think she's hiding there but we didn't want to lead anyone to her until we found out why she is hiding, so we couldn't stop. Something's wrong with her, Ira. She needs help."

"You want me to go in and get her?" He understood immediately. "I can bring her to Sara. We'll take care of her."

Suddenly they were startled by a burst of Portuguese maledictions delivered in a fierce quarrelsome tone. Petrina turned and saw Catarina facing the heavy-set man as he would have walked out on the dock.

"*Não!*" Catarina shouted at him.

He tried frantically to walk around her but she seized a handful of his shirt in one hand while she braced herself against her cane, continuing to upbraid him at the top of her voice.

"I'll go into Miami as soon as you folks get out of here," Ira promised quickly. "As soon as I can, I'll let you know how it's going."

"Not over the telephone."

Ira's eyebrows beetled down. "He used to listen when *she* made calls, too. Sara told me."

"If you have to leave a message you can trust Marinta. Or David and Catarina."

"My God, somebody peel this crazy foreigner off me!" the heavy-set man shouted desperately at David, who shrugged, at Ira and Petrina.

Catarina, seeing that Petrina had attended to her business with Ira, released the shirt and stood staring up at the man's flushed face. With formidable dignity she asked icily, "Who do you call crazy foreigner?" She eyed him with contempt as he backed away from her. "You want to walk on dock, walk on dock," she directed magnanimously.

"Your boat looks good," Petrina complimented as Ira walked back to David's car with her.

Ira's faded eyes twinkled as they paused to look at the skifflike boat, its paint mottled and scarred, every blemish revealed by the glaring sunlight. Its 150-horsepower aviation engine and five-foot propeller loomed high behind the wire cage that separated his power source from the two high chairs mounted one behind another for operator and one passenger.

"It'll do," Ira said dryly. "Ain't much for looks but it'll get Sara and me anywhere we want to go back in there and carry still another with us."

"Thank you, Ira. Maybe next time I'll be able to take you up on your invitation. Give me a rain check, would you?"

They took off down the Trail again, their green tail following behind, and turned north when they reached Carnestown. The green car remained behind when they passed through Cypress Glade and continued on to the big silvery Victorian house that waited in the humid heat of late afternoon out on its isolated hammock.

Marinta bustled forward with complete delight when she saw still another guest in tow. Her pleasure was genuine, though she was concerned at how Senhora Régio was to manage the stairs.

"For this one weekend?" Catarina scoffed. "I manage! You see!"

Once Marinta had the elderly psychic settled into her bedroom for a recuperative nap, however, Marinta drew Petrina hurriedly off to her room.

"Things been going on here while you been away!" Marinta announced. "You got to start looking around your room here and see is there something missing!"

Petrina began to examine her possessions, opening drawers in the big dresser, checking one after another from the small glove drawers below the mirror to the big drawers at the very bottom. Nothing appeared to be

disarranged. "Why am I looking at everything?" she
asked. "What am I looking for?"

"I don't for the life of me know." Marinta sat her bulk
down on the edge of the bed. "I was working downstairs,
getting that little breakfast room cleaned out so you folks
could be eating there, and all of the sudden I hears the
telephone ring. I drop what I'm doing and start out toward the front of the house to answer, and then it stops. I
hear him talking up there in the hall. Then he comes
downstairs like he's going to get something in the study,
only when he goes back upstairs he doesn't have anything
in his hand. So he is just looking to see I'm not on the telephone, too. That's what I think. He talk a little bit more
on the telephone up there and then he hang up."

Petrina was listening intently, continuing to search,
this time in her closet. First the upper shelf where she
was keeping her shoes and a few bulky shawls. One by
one she pushed hangers along, checking dresses.

"All of a sudden," Marinta went on dramatically, "I
hears creaking where there wasn't supposed to be any.
Up where our rooms are, where he doesn't have any business poking around."

With a swift motion Petrina crossed the room and
pulled the case in which she kept Peter and the Pedlar
doll out from under her dressing table where she had
pushed them this morning. She opened the lid of the carrying case and pulled Peter out, sitting him in the corner
of the big upholstered chair in the corner. She knew she
was stalling, that she was afraid of what she would find.

"You got the doll fixed!" Marinta exclaimed, looking
past her into the carrying case. "I sure am glad of that!"

Petrina reached down and picked up the Pedlar doll,
felt its scarlet skirt billow out over her hand, felt the tension of the ribbons hold the tray out away from the body

offering its selection of wares. She looked at the wares and shivered. Instead of the pewter goblet, silver thimble, the velvet cap with its substitute ornament carefully glued on, instead—she was looking at a completely different tray of wares. This doll had a dozen little baskets of varying sizes, pillows, tiny packets of pins, minute books with thin ribbon markers.

"Miss Gentry, do you feel all right?" Marinta's voice seemed to come from a long way off.

This doll was a totally different doll. Its beautiful white leather face was kindly, its mouth curved in a faint smile. It was the doll she had chosen back at Mr. Conolly's shop, the doll Mr. Tyron had carried through customs.

"Where is Mr. Addison now?" Petrina asked.

Marinta's eyes were wide. "He went out right after I heard him up in your room, and he was carrying something in a big brown paper grocery bag. About ten minutes later, back he came carrying the same brown paper bag. He went upstairs again and after a while he went back out and that time he wasn't carrying anything. That's why I wanted you to be sure to look over everything in your room. Something funny is going on."

It wasn't hard to figure out what happened.

With Tony's cooperation, Tyron had finally managed to engineer the exchange of the dolls.

"You're right about something going on," Petrina sighed. "Only it isn't all that funny, Marinta. Was Mr. Addison in your room at all?"

A faintly scandalized look skipped across Marinta's wide black face. "No, Miss Gentry. He was not."

Petrina made an effort to bring order to her thoughts. "I'm going to have to keep my appointment with Mr. Brock—it's for late this afternoon. I make that to be four-thirty. When Senhora Régio wakes up, would you fix her a cup of tea or a drink or whatever she wants and some muffins or cookies. Whatever you can think of nice. I'll be back about five-thirty or six. If Ira calls, please take a message."

"Best you take your Mr. Nairac along with you," Marinta advised positively.

Petrina ran a brush through her tousled hair and looked herself over critically. She needed color. She looked tired and frightened and psyching herself up for the coming encounter with Mr. Brock would not work to conceal the ravages of anxiety and strain. She opened her theatrical makeup box and did a hurried expert job on her cheeks and lips and eyelids.

"I wouldn't have believed it," Marinta complimented admiringly. "Just a little paint and a little skill and you look like you slept a week and you going to a party!"

"Thank goodness for that!"

Petrina ran downstairs and found David browsing through some of the books in the study.

"Would you please come along with me for my appointment with Mr. Brock?" she asked abruptly.

His dark eyes were suddenly very soft on her. "Of course I'll go with you. We'll take my car, if you don't mind."

Tony was pulling into the parking place in front of the house as they walked out onto the porch. His blue eyes were maliciously bright and triumphant.

"We'll be back in about an hour," Petrina told him. "I want to talk to you."

"Don't hurry." He smiled. "I'll have the ice cubes all ready for action by the time you get back. Have a nice visit with our good counselor-at-law."

He was very pleased with the clever coup he had executed against her and no doubt he had been well paid. There was nothing she could say to help him either. Very soon Tyron would discover he had been given a fake stone and Tony would find himself a player in a much bigger and uglier game than he had anticipated.

Heavy banks of clouds were climbing the sky to the southwest and a glowering shudder of lightning radiation illuminated a large area violently, symbolically.

CHAPTER 18

David's face was somber as he negotiated the rutted lane down to the road into Cypress Glade. He had listened carefully to her account of Tony's prowling and the substituted doll.

"By now Tyron knows he's been had," David mused. "He'll be back. You know that. We can't plan that Julian's men will be here or how they will be able to help if they do get here. If it becomes necessary to turn the diamond over to him, Trina, if he is armed and we have no choice, you'll have to do it promptly and without guilt."

"No!" Petrina's voice was tight and angry. "Give it to him so he can sell it and they can set off more bombs and kill more people? Not on your life, David! We've got to have more choices than that!"

He did not reply. They had very few choices and they both knew it.

A few sprinkles of rain spattered on the windshield.

"Sam Brock's office is off to the left at the next turn. Two doors down in that long cement-block building over there."

He made the turn and parked on the sandy area in front of the structure. A big water oak towered above, deflecting the sparse raindrops, but a heavy spear of lightning toward the west followed by a heavy percussion of thunder warned that more than a light shower was on the way.

Nothing had changed about Sam Brock's office, except

that he had annexed the narrow store that used to sell a limited stock of hardware items, Petrina saw. Sam Brock looked much the same too, she discovered, as they entered the cluttered office. The secretary's space was still up front where she could intercept his clients before they got back to his glassed-in cubicle. But she had evidently left early. It was Mrs. Brock who occupied the chair drawn up at the secretary's desk.

Sam Brock was hunched over papers strewn on his oversized fancy desk top. His heavy porcine face bent down as though he were unaware that anyone had entered his outer office. Like the mean wild feral Everglades hogs he resembled, Brock was volatile and dangerous, and, like them, aware of every changing air current when the change affected him.

"We thought maybe you were so tired from your trip into Miami you might have decided to cancel your appointment here," Mrs. Brock sniffed, her face mirroring a peculiar mixture of curiosity and apprehension.

There was no hesitancy in Sam Brock's manner as he called out, "Just come right in here, folks, and sit down." He dragged forward two worn captain's chairs that had been against the wall and placed them in front of his desk. As his wife stood uncertainly in the doorway of the cubicle he gave her an impatient wave of the hand. "You go on home now and get supper started. I'll be there directly."

So he didn't expect the interview to take very long, Petrina surmised. After his wife had scurried through the outer office and the front door, Brock turned to Petrina and there was nothing pleasant in his small bloodshot eyes, though he continued to smile.

"You gave my man quite a chase in the city today," he admitted jovially. "He had a terrible time keeping up with you folks."

"If you'd told me you were having someone follow us we could have made it easier for him," Petrina returned coolly. "We didn't know he was your man. Why did you send him? Did you think we might know where Linette was and that we wouldn't tell you?"

He no longer smiled. "She did cable you. If she had gotten in touch, you might not have let me know."

Petrina started to get to her feet.

"Did she get in touch?" Brock demanded, his voice soft yet very threatening.

"No." She settled back in the chair. "You must know she didn't. Your man was behind us wherever we went."

"You spent some time driving around the neighborhood where your aunt used to live, I was told. Why should you do that when nobody around here has even thought about it since your aunt died? It was listed with a Miami real estate outfit. The place was empty, run-down, no utilities—but did you maybe expect to find your cousin hiding out there?"

This time Petrina did stand up. "I came over here to see if you might know something that could help, but there's no point in talking to you," she snapped. "You and Tony have become paranoid. I don't know why she cabled me for help or why she's hiding from you but I'm determined to find out when I see her."

Brock smiled triumphantly. "That may be sooner than you think, Miss Gentry. When Leonard told me you were snooping around the old neighborhood I realized we hadn't given that place the attention we should have. We had it checked once and when she wasn't there we let it go. That was apparently our mistake. I sent him right back there as fast as he could move to see what was going on and if there was any sign she'd been there, to make sure he brought her back when he came."

Petrina kept any trace of shock from registering on her

face, grateful for the training that made her able to conceal as well as to project expression.

"You really are paranoid, aren't you, Mr. Brock?" She tucked her handbag under her arm. "I was hoping you'd tell me what you and Tony were working on with the oil company and whether that might have had something to do with Linette's disappearance—but I can see you aren't going to do that, are you?"

David unfolded his length from his own chair. "You'll let us know as soon as you hear anything, won't you, Mr. Brock?"

Brock let them see themselves out of his office without even voicing a good-by. Though he had turned away from them, Petrina saw that his face was flushed with anger. He was having a hard time maintaining control of himself, and he was determined to keep them from seeing the full measure of his discomposure. The telephone on his desk began to ring. He made no move to pick it up as they walked through the outer office and out onto the street.

A burst of cold wind-driven rain caught at them as they stepped out. In the short space of time they had been inside, the sky had darkened and the clouds had begun to empty in the sudden downpour characteristic of the onset of storms in the subtropical rainy season.

When they had gained the shelter of David's car, Petrina gasped. "David, he doesn't know what Tony's been up to on his own, does he? Tony didn't tell him about Tyron and the doll!"

David turned the ignition key. "We'd better hope he didn't," he replied grimly. "We don't want Brock joining forces with Tyron!"

The rain drummed against the metal of the car roof and the windshield wipers batted valiantly against the flow of blinding water. David reduced the powerful car's speed to a crawl as the headlights cast a wavering glow upon the streaming roadbed without penetrating the solid curtain of water blowing at them. It was only six o'clock but it might as well have been dusk.

Petrina tried desperately to spot the turnoff for the house, leaning forward in a fruitless effort to see through the windshield.

"It's all right," David reassured her. "I know where we are. I won't have any trouble finding the turn."

Her eyes flashed up to his, meeting them for an instant and dropping away before he could see the doubt in them.

He chuckled softly, the sound muffled by the noise of the rain. "There's no need to worry, really." As though to prove what he had said, he turned the steering wheel and after a momentary shuddering the wheels of the big car gained purchase sending a great fan of water sheeting off a wide puddle that covered any demarcation of road.

At last a tall jagged structure loomed up through the gray screen of rain. David parked directly in front of the entrance to the porch and turned off the lights and the motor. For a moment they sat motionless, listening to the rain, letting the tension of the struggle drain away.

"Darned if you didn't do it," she admitted, finally.

His pleased grin of acknowledgment was strangely youthful. "Ready to make a run for it?"

"I don't think we'll have to."

With a wild flap, nerve-racking as the launching flight of a condor, Marinta dashed out into the downpour unfurling a huge black umbrella under which she conveyed them to shelter. Throughout the noisy confusion Tony Addison remained to the side watching, glass in his hand, blue eyes coldly aware, aloof, still triumphant. Catarina was ensconced in a graceful wicker chair whose arching oval back behind her black-clad figure framed her like some medieval queen. Her ebony eyes were intense and alert though her manner was composed.

A flare of lightning glared across the windows to the east, outlining the dwarfed reaching limbs of a bald cypress near the house and splitting with a sharp crack the tall exposed length of a pine farther out. Almost simultaneously a shock wave of thunder shook the air.

"Por Deus do ceu!" Catarina breathed.

The electricity went out, leaving the room in a darkness peopled with vague gray aftershapes. A few seconds later, after a few false blinks, the lights came back on. The big overhead fan, slowed almost to a halt by its loss of power, resumed the soft slow whup of its motions.

Marinta brought in kerosene lamps and distributed them about the living room, lighted one for insurance. The acrid smell of ozone from the lightning strike drifted in wisps across the room and was as quickly dissipated.

Slowly the storm moved from directly overhead and as the battering crashes of thunder and the hard slash of rain against the windows began to fade, they became aware of the telephone ringing back in Tony's study.

With a soft expletive he pushed past Marinta and dashed down the hallway. When he came back he regarded Petrina curiously. "That is Mrs. Brock on the phone," he informed her without ceremony. "She said Sam never got back home and she wondered if you knew anything about it."

"He was there when we left and it had already begun to storm," Petrina returned. "The telephone was ringing. I suppose he was waiting until we were gone to answer it. Maybe he's just waiting out the storm instead of going out into it."

"She tried to reach him at his office. There was no answer."

"Why on earth are you so concerned?" Petrina asked

with interest. "He's a big boy. I'm sure he can find his way home in Cypress Glade, of all places."

"I'll tell her you can't help her," Tony said lamely and went back to the telephone.

A quiet chill tongue of fear moved over Petrina's skin as a new thought struck her. If Sam Brock's man was shrewd enough to bring to Sam Brock's attention the fact that they had been driving through Aunt Ellen's old neighborhood, sooner or later he would have questioned the significance of their visit later to the airboat dock and their conversation with Ira.

Even if Ira had managed to reach Linette and persuade her to go away with him, she would not be safe for long once Sam Brock made the connection. The telephone call Brock waited to answer in his office might have been from his man calling from Miami to tell Brock their quarry had gone to ground.

With the storm beginning to slacken, time was running out. Sam Brock was born and bred in this part of the state. He might choose to dodge the discomfort of the height of the storm, but the trailing edges would not delay him.

"Catarina." Petrina spoke softly.

The Portuguese psychic's head turned to Petrina and the obsidian eyes were shocking in the power of their concentration. "*Sim?*"

"I'm going to make a run out tonight and I'd like to take David with me. I don't want Tony to know where I've gone. Would you stay here and keep him occupied for a while?"

"*Sim.*" A faint ironic smile curved Catarina's lips. "You think better I should not know where you go or how or why, and perhaps you are right. I can say I do not know much more convincingly when I have not been told."

"Thank you." Petrina looked up at David's saturnine face and read in its perceptive concern that he was worried too. "They'll think of Ira, David. I've got to get to him first. Will you come with me? Now?"

"If I thought it might make you change your mind about venturing out, I'd say no. But it wouldn't. Of course I'll go with you." He grinned. "I hope to heaven you can run an airboat, though. I can't."

"Ira was a good teacher. I think I can get us there safely." She hurried along, her mind occupied with the realities ahead. "Rain ponchos used to be kept out in the storeroom in back of the kitchen—let's hope they still are."

Marinta was just pulling a pan of hot rolls from the oven as they burst into the kitchen.

Petrina paused only to pull open an end cabinet drawer and withdraw a couple of flashlights, test them, hand one to David. "Please serve Senhora Régio and Mr. Addison their dinners, Marinta, and tell them we'll be back very shortly. We had to go out."

Marinta nodded briskly and her round face hardened with resolution. "I understand, Miss Gentry. Any message if Mr. Ira comes back?"

"I hope there won't have to be a message."

It answered Marinta's unspoken question. She raised her hand in acknowledgment and went back to her chores as Petrina closed the door behind herself and waved David toward the storeroom.

There were two full-size ponchos hanging from nails near the door leading directly outside from the storeroom. David reached them down, shaking an accumulation of dust from them and limbering some of the stiffness hanging had put in their folds.

"We don't have time for that!" Petrina scolded impatiently, pulling her own poncho down over her head and snapping herself into it. David followed suit and they stepped outside, pulling the hoods up for protection.

The storm was far from over. Although the rain was not slashing at them anymore, it was coming down hard enough to blot out everything but the nearest vegetation. They hadn't gone more than a few yards when several rotted-out creases in the ponchos began to let in the first of many cold wet leaks. She slipped several times in the slick grasses tufting part of the narrow path and heard a couple of heavy thumps behind her as David lost his footing, too.

"There's the dock, right up ahead there. There ought to be some extra gas in some cans under the shed."

"My God, it's dark out here," David marveled.

"Good thing," she returned. "It will slow us down a lot and it will slow Brock, but not nearly enough. It won't slow Ira, though, so the advantage will be his."

She jerked the protective tarp off the airboat and began to check it over.

"Is this the boat Linette took off in when she disappeared?" David asked, looking it over himself. "It doesn't seem to have been in an accident and injured, does it?"

The bumper at the front was solidly in place. It would ride smoothly over the tallest saw grass. Rudders at the back had not been damaged. Throttle was all right, still attached to the cable connecting it to the motor. The battery wires to the fuel pump were secure. The gasoline tank held a little more than twenty-five gallons of aviation fuel when it was full. She didn't want to waste time checking how much was in it now. David lifted two fifteen-gallon spare cans of gasoline aboard for emergency.

"This is rigged so I sit up front, passenger behind," she told him. "Climb aboard, passenger." She scrambled up into the high chair and turned on the ignition and went limp with relief momentarily as it fired off with no trouble.

"I'm pretty good out here but it wouldn't do any harm if you keep your direction thoughts turned on," she called to David. "I'm not going to turn on the boat lights until we're well away from here, just in case."

She came down hard on the throttle lever under her foot and felt the light boat spring forward, driving the rain stingingly against her skin. The rudders responded smoothly to her pressure on the steering bar.

CHAPTER 19

Petrina set her course due north, checking the battered compass set in the boat's control box from time to time with the beam of her flashlight. When she had traveled some ten minutes out from the home dock so it was unlikely she might have been seen and somehow followed, she switched on her boat light. The light was more a psychological than an actual help on a night like this.

On this black night especially there was no way to tell the curve of the earth, no horizon that could set some sort of boundary. Skimming over the vast stretches of high saw grass, there was no way to set reference points—as Ira had told her when he first took her out, the only way to keep from getting lost was to remember exactly where you were, as well as where you wanted to go.

After a brief calm interval, the wind picked up again, laying the saw grass down in winnowed fashion and blending weirdly the water of the swamp with the pouring rain. She throttled the motor down to minimize the bite of the rain.

"You still there, passenger?" she called back to David.

She saw his teeth flash white in a smile. "Just a minute. I'll see," he shouted back.

"Hold on, passenger!" She eased the boat to the left, where a path of matted saw grass showed that boats frequently made their way here. "This is where Ira likes to gig frogs. He used to take Linette and me here to gig for our suppers. Ira's camp is on Lost Hammock, up north-northwest about ten minutes from here."

They were both chilled and tired when she swept the airboat up to Ira's primitive dock and tied it to a post. Ira's boat was tied to the other side, she saw, and she sighed with release of anxiety when it was apparent that theirs were the only boats.

Shouting at the top of her voice, she stood on the end of the dock without moving toward land until she saw the swinging light of a lantern and heard an answering shout.

Ira was standing in the doorway of a rough fishing shack, built shotgun style to catch the prevailing wind all the way through. He held out his arms to her and she rushed to hug him.

"I've been expecting you," he said. "It came to me just about the time I was halfway home with Linette that Sam Brock might not be near as stupid as I thought. Sara's inside. You still like frog legs?" He stepped aside so they could walk in.

Tears caught in Petrina's throat as she looked past the homemade chairs Ira had built for the living room, the big coquina-rock fireplace with its blackened maw filled with pine tufts and cypress, the big bed set in the middle of the room and beyond, the long plank table in the kitchen area, where Sara, tiny and indomitable, ruled unchallenged. Strung along the walls were chains of drying herbs and grasses, leaves, branches of tiny hot bird peppers. The aroma enfolded her gently as she moved forward, pulling her wet poncho up over her head and dropping it on the floor beside the door. Behind her, David did the same.

"Sara—"

The tiny woman jabbed fiercely at the tears that ran

down her cheeks. "Thank God you're back," she cried, and Petrina saw suddenly why she hadn't come forward. One foot was encased in a plaster cast and she was clearly numbering her movements. When she saw Petrina's expression she hurriedly sniffed, "It's just about knit and healed now. No need to worry."

"Linette—"

The blond girl at the table looked up at her blankly, as though the name Petrina spoke meant nothing to her.

"She's been like that ever since Ira brought her here." Sara moved away from the table and Petrina was able to clearly see her cousin, the woman for whom Petrina's fiancé had left her, for the first time in a year.

The fragile thin face was still startlingly beautiful but Linette's long blond hair was unkempt and it needed washing. Tangled in the silky matted strands were bits of twigs and straw and what seemed to be a leaf. She was still wearing the faded shirt and jeans in which Petrina had last seen her, and beneath them, she could see now, Linette's body was shockingly thin.

This deterioration had not come about in just the time since Linette had been missing. Something had gone very wrong for Linette for a long time and her husband had apparently done nothing to help her. If indeed he had not been the cause. The untidy emaciated girl who dropped her head abruptly upon her arms was only a shadow of the lovely fastidious Linette of a year ago.

Petrina felt herself catapulted back three years to when she first had lost her father, when she had first come to Cypress Glade and Aunt Ellen and Linette and Ira and Sara. She had been physically used up after Robert Gentry's long final illness. Raw from loss and emotional pain she had gone numbly inside herself. Like Linette now, she had been lost and alone for a while and the wall she had erected between herself and the others had been all but impenetrable for a long long time. Like this terrible wall with which Linette had encased and protected herself.

With a sharp sob, she turned away and felt David's arms hold her tight against the comforting warmth of his body. David had understood this quality about her, the lost frightened child, the angry unforgiving child when Linette had married Tony.

In many ways they were much alike, she and Linette, for all their differences. But Robert Gentry had been able to give Petrina something Linette had not had, an introduction to a different world into which she could step from the world of Cypress Glade. And more important than anything else in the world, there had been David, David who had stepped into her life and who had become her world.

David's arms dropped away from her even as she was thinking about him. But before the contact broke she felt a surge of joyful elation rock him, and felt it amplified by every receptive echoing cell in her own body.

Involuntarily she cried out and dimly heard his voice whisper roughly, unevenly, "It's all right, Trina. It's all right, darling." He took a deep ragged breath and she sensed a turbulence subside in him.

"It happens that way sometimes." He was no more in command of himself than she was, at this moment. "In my work I am trained to listen to thoughts that are not spoken, to emotions that are not recognized—to all the range of extrasensory communication. I promised you I would not do that with you unless you permitted it—but we were very close, Trina. I did not realize what was happening in time. I'm sorry."

She was astonished to see by both Ira and Sara's faces, both exhibiting only concern for Linette, that neither had been aware of the exchange between David and herself.

"Is there anything you can do to help her?" she asked David, forcing her thoughts away from David and toward Linette.

"She will need psychiatric help for a time, for recovery. Quiet. Relief from the pressure she has been under."

Sara nodded emphatically. "She has to get away from *him*."

"Him" had to be Tony. Ira got a leather handbag from the counter alongside Sara's cookstove. "She wouldn't come with me until she climbed up into the attic of the Miami house and got this and brought it along. I asked her what was in it and she didn't answer. She didn't seem to know."

"She knew."

Linette lifted her head at the sound of David's deep pleasant voice. For the first time she appeared to be at all aware of her surroundings and that people were around her. She reached out and snatched the handbag from Ira's hand and put her head down again, this time pillowed on the purse.

"I'd like to try something. I think it's important."

David pulled out a chair and sat down beside the girl, taking her hand in his. "You wanted to see Petrina, didn't you?" He had to ask the question twice before she made any response, and even then it was not verbal. Linette gave a slight nod without raising her head.

"You found something." It was not a question he asked.

She nodded.

"It was a paper. A legal paper. And you knew Petrina must have it and that it would destroy your life."

Tears gathered and slowly rolled from the closed eyes. David took both her hands in his.

"Everything will be all right," he told her, his voice authoritative, kindly, penetrating the armor around her with its message. "Petrina loves you. She is here. Ira and Sara are here. We will take care of you."

She took a deep ragged breath and suddenly, amazingly, her body relaxed and like an exhausted youngster, she was asleep. David picked her up and carried her over to the big bed and laid her gently down. He went back and got the handbag and gave it to Petrina.

"She was guarding this for you," he said. "You'd better take a look at it."

From the handbag Petrina drew a will, typed on legal paper, with the customary notations. It was dated just a little more than a year ago, a week or two at most before Aunt Ellen had died. Petrina's knees went weak and she sank down on one of the kitchen chairs to read. One time she read each word of the legalese, trying to decipher exactly what was being said, a second time she read it again to absorb each word in order to realize that it was true.

Aunt Ellen had left her estate to be equally divided between her nieces and had left explicit instructions as to just how that division was to take place. But that was not what left Petrina shocked, her heart pumping to drive warming blood through her chilled body. The will had been drawn up by Sam Brock and witnessed by his wife and Tony Addison.

Aunt Ellen had not had time before she died to prepare Linette for the change in the will's provisions and inform her of it in a way that would not threaten Linette. Perhaps she had intended to do so when she met Linette in Miami, with the change an accomplished fact.

Then came that terrible crash on the way to Miami. Had the handbag been on the seat beside her when the car left the road? And had the handbag been lost in the crash, found later, returned to Linette?

Petrina looked over at the frail sleeping woman with her bruised blue eyelids hiding the horror behind them. She had read the will and discovered that her own husband had knowingly teamed with her lawyer to make her an unwitting partner in the estate fraud. Linette must have been stunned when she read the document and realized what was going on. Had she argued with them? Threatened them?

No wonder Brock and Addison were beside themselves with fear and anger. They had known the will existed and Sam Brock knew that Aunt Ellen had taken all of the copies of the new will with her, instead of leaving the original in his office, as she had done with the first one, keeping only the duplicates. Perhaps by then she had begun to distrust him and he knew it.

What they dreaded most must have materialized when Linette confronted them with her knowledge and refused to surrender the documents to them. Her retreat into a fortress of silence had left them with a legal time bomb.

That part did not matter now. Linette would work her way back out of the nightmare into which she had been thrust and in due time the answers would all be given.

"Please put this in your pocket." Petrina handed the will to David, glad to have it out of her own hands.

Ira cocked his head alertly, ear toward the open door. Past the spattering sound of rain against the porch roof they could hear the faraway roar of an airboat. Ira walked to the rack above the front door and took down a shotgun, broke it and shoved a cartridge into the breach, closed it. "Brock," he informed them. "I know the sound of his boat. I'll get on out there to welcome him. When he yells, you just invite him up."

He stepped out into the darkness and disappeared soundlessly into the undergrowth. Nobody spoke as the sound of the airboat sped closer and finally stopped at the dock in front. Brock shouted his arrival. From inside the house Sara shouted back as Ira had instructed.

Both boats were visible to Brock as he pulled up. He would have known whom to expect at the camp. They heard the sound of his footsteps, just one set, so he hadn't brought anyone with him, stumping up the wet pathway, slapping on the two steps leading up to the shallow porch. He had a cocked handgun in his hand as he stepped through the door and his porcine face in the light of the kerosene lamps was folded in ugly malevolent creases.

"You had to come here, didn't you?" he growled at Petrina. "You had to stick your nose into business that didn't concern you. Well, now you found her for us. I'm going to take her back to her husband and you had better not try to stop me." He looked around uneasily as nobody spoke. "Where is Ira?"

"Right here behind you."

As Brock swung around Ira brought the stock of the shotgun smashing solidly against the lawyer's skull. Brock swayed and crashed down like a great animal, shaking the floor and joggling for a moment the flame from the kerosene lamp on the table. Ira rubbed the stock of the gun stolidly and stepped over Brock's body. "It was that or shoot him," he explained as Sara looked at him in shocked reproof. "At this range shooting him would have killed him."

Sara nodded, looking down at the lawyer's body with disgust.

"We have to get out of here in case the other one comes," Ira said. "First I'm going to run his boat on out a ways so it won't be seen and he won't be able to get at it if he comes to after we leave. You come out behind me, Trina, and bring me back here. Then Sara and I will bring Linette along with us in our boat and you and David follow in yours. We'll go back to your house and work from there."

He reached down the other gun from over the doorway, a rifle, and handed it to Sara. The fallen gun that had dropped from Brock's hand he gave to David, who slid it into his pocket.

"You going to leave him here?" Sara inquired. She was busily putting small packets of dried crushed leaves into her apron pockets. "Untied?"

Ira nodded. "Where can he go without a boat? He may not deserve it but at least this way he can survive in case anything happens to us."

"Remember to turn out the light then behind us when it's time to go so he doesn't have a chance to burn the place down," she sniffed.

CHAPTER 20

No illusions cheered Petrina as she followed Ira's lead boat across the trackless river of grass. The realities were far too apparent. Catarina was capable of distracting Tony's attention for a while. But two women, one elderly and not physically strong, the other a black servant past her own youthful strength, could not hold out against Tony without help, not if he were determined. Certainly they could not hold out if the Australian joined with him in an effort to find the diamond.

Petrina tried to imagine how a man would feel when the house of his deception began to collapse about him one crumbling piece at a time. Desperate, she thought. Enraged. Frightened. A man who felt like this would stop at nothing. He would have nothing to lose and he would fight like any trapped animal for whatever it appeared to him he could salvage.

Up ahead Ira's shoulders were hunched over his tiller as he concentrated on reading his course across the rippling grass. Behind him Sara and Linette huddled together.

The rain was coming down harder now, and the wind had a sharper sweep after they left the protective windbreak of the hammock. The wind thrust had quartered and overhead the massed clouds began a wide diffused flashing that threw eerie shadowing and echoing afterscenes. A scorching javelin of light speared down into a nearby stand of trees, destroying several in two swift thrusts followed by a blast as stunning as a bomb explosion. Petrina screamed but her voice was lost in the concussion of thunder.

Ira's boat light signaled, a pale glimmer after the flare of lightning. They were getting close to the dock. It was time to throttle down.

At least with the storm back again in force, it was unlikely that anyone at the house would hear them.

The dim outlines of Ira's boat slipped up to the outthrust finger of dock and Petrina watched as Ira leaped out and helped Sara and then went back to get Linette. The three started up the path and Petrina brought her own boat in and tethered it next to Ira's. David hurried her along the dock, trying unsuccessfully to shield her from the wind with his own body.

The back of the house was dark as they approached it. Ira and the two women had let themselves into the storeroom and were waiting there in the dark when Petrina and David entered. Petrina gasped as Sara's hand groped and touched her. The noise of the storm was muted by the closed door but it might still cover any inadvertent sound they might make. Petrina gestured with her flashlight toward the door to the kitchen.

Leaving their wet ponchos behind on the floor of the storeroom, they moved cautiously into the pantry. No one was in the kitchen and the light was not on. Petrina sent a quick beam of light toward the sink. Dishes with bits of food on them dried on the sideboard and nearby cooking utensils were left carelessly piled, unemptied. Marinta could not abide a messy kitchen. She had not been able to complete her dinner cleanup.

From the family living room came a faint sound of raised voices, interrupted by a rumble of thunder. David's fingers bit into Petrina's arm and she heard his sharp indrawn breath and knew he was afraid for her.

Enough light spilled from the open living room door so they could see their way down the hallway. Petrina glanced back and was relieved to glimpse Linette lagging behind at the kitchen door, staring about dreamily. Ira was carrying the shotgun, Sara the rifle. David drew his captured gun from his pocket but he was frowning, glancing about.

He was uneasy about something but she couldn't ask and he could not tell her what it was.

They were almost to the lighted doorway, Ira with his gun cocked at ready, when a feminine voice spoke from just inside the darkened formal living room across the hallway.

"Lay your arms down where you are, good people, and go right in. We've been expecting you. Please don't be foolish. Tyron has you covered."

Slowly Petrina turned. "Morag!"

The Irish girl moved with catlike dancer's grace from her hiding place and waved them on. Morag was wearing jeans with a scarlet jersey and her pale eyes glittered. In her hand she held, incredibly, a small wax doll, crudely fashioned, barely recognizable as a doll.

From the doll's head thrust a few wisps of brown hair. Its dress was a snippet of material the same yellow as one of Petrina's favorite dresses. Petrina's eyes widened and for a moment she didn't breathe, remembering the day Morag had gone to her dressing room when she wasn't there and Katy had seen her handling brushes, other things.

"So you know about dolls like this," Morag said, her pale eyes narrowing. "David knows about dolls like this, too. And Catarina."

"Morag, don't do this," David said, his voice rough, his face ashen.

"Of course I will," Morag sneered. "We will all sit

down and have a nice talk. And that little twit of yours will tell me exactly what she did with the stone we went to so bloody much trouble to get our hands on. She will tell or I will destroy her. My God—" For an instant her eyes raged with a fury that was close to madness. "Do you realize what we went through to get that diamond? Then to get it and have that fool Conolly trick us with the dolls? And then you—"

She waved them into the family room.

Ira and Sara arranged themselves side by side alongside Marinta, while across from them sat Catarina, her face impassive ivory, only her brilliant jet eyes alive. Tony was slumped at a cluttered game table, part of what was happening, yet detached from it too. Abruptly Petrina found her knees too weak to carry her farther into the room and she sank down on a chair just inside the doorway. David had stopped too, and was standing beside her.

Morag held up the crude wax doll, dangling it by a red thread tied around its throat. Her dancer's body swayed rhythmically as though to the beat of music only she could hear.

"Explain to her what will happen to her if she doesn't tell us what we want to know," Morag said softly, her eyes on David.

Catarina spat out several words in Portuguese, then said carefully in English, "You were unwise to let us come together in this room. You do not learn from your mistakes."

"I have the power to hurt her with this." Morag held out the doll. "I can kill her, if I choose. With this doll or with Tyron's gun. It makes no difference to me. Where is that stone, Petrina?" Petrina felt the malignity in Morag's eyes strike out like shards of pale glass.

The room seemed to go still, the air electric with a

force as real as the lightning crackling beyond the window.

Morag stepped back, her eyes wild. "No!" she screamed, looking from David to Catarina.

Marinta's hands clasped together and her eyes were wide with fear. Her lips were moving, as though in prayer.

Morag's fingers went toward the doll again, curving like talons that were held back by invisible restraints from tearing at the simulacrum.

From back in the kitchen area came the distant sound of a metal utensil falling to the floor and rolling. Petrina's eyes flew to Sara's. Linette.

Tyron stepped through the doorway far enough to train his gun down the hall. "What the hell was that?" he snarled.

"A cat," Sara answered promptly. "Always kept a cat here."

"Where is everybody?" Linette's light voice hung on the air as disembodied as a ghost. "Why did you leave me alone out there?" A frightened frantic edge came into it. "I don't want to be alone any more!"

"Come on in here, then," Tyron called back, his lip curling in an ugly smile. "We'll take care of you, lady. You won't be alone. We're in the parlor."

Petrina saw Tony's body tense as Tyron's grin took on a predatory arrogance while he peered down the hallway.

"Well, well—now why is a pretty little thing like you being kept out there in the kitchen? You just come in here and I'll be glad to keep you company."

Tyron jerked Linette up against him as she walked dazedly through the doorway.

"She's my wife!" Tony's agonized howl brought Tyron's head around. "Leave her be!"

"Is she now?" Tyron sneered. "She's the one that ran

away from you? Maybe it's a good man she's been looking for, eh?"

With a scream of rage Tony hurled himself from his
chair and catapulted across the room toward Tyron.
Coolly, without changing expression, Tyron brought his
gun down on a line with Tony's chest and pulled the trigger. Tony jerked and hung in the air for a moment,
caught in midleap, before he crashed to the floor.

Held by Tyron's tensed arm, Linette made a stifled
small sound of horror and collapsed, dangling like some
boneless mindless bit of flesh. With a grunt of disgust,
Tyron let her drop. "Anyone else want to try me?" he
demanded.

Morag's eyes stared past him at Petrina. "I want that
stone." The elemental passion in her voice seemed to link
her with the storm blowing itself out beyond the window.
"I stole for that stone. I killed for it. The money I get for
it is going to blow away thousands of *Sassenachs* for me!
Where did you put that diamond?"

"I won't tell you!" Petrina screamed back. "You can
stick all the pins you want to into that stupid doll and it
won't matter to me! You have to have credence in super-
stitions to make them work and I don't believe in witchcraft!"

Morag's eyes went wide in stunned disbelief as she
tried desperately to bring her other hand to the doll and
found that no matter how she tried, she could not do it.

Catarina's black eyes did not move from the Irish girl.
"Release the doll," Catarina ordered sharply. "Open your
fingers and drop it."

Morag threw back her head. "No!" she shrieked. The
full venom of her glance focused on Petrina. "You fool!
You fool!" Her eyes pinned Tyron. "Shoot her!" she
screamed. "She isn't going to tell us what we want to
know anyhow!"

Tyron pointed the gun that had already taken one life

that night and Petrina looked into the darkness of the barrel, smelled the sharp acrid odor of spent gunpowder. Tyron's finger was tightening on the trigger.

He was smiling, a tight cruel smile. He would enjoy this assignment. She had meant defeat for him from the moment he had encountered her in London and putting an end to her would even the score. To him she was only a small-time little ventriloquist who didn't have sense enough to keep out of political games where she was hopelessly outclassed.

At his feet Linette stirred. He glanced down, pushed her body farther away with his foot. His finger on the trigger of the gun remained steady.

The paralysis of fear that had frozen Petrina broke with that second of distraction and she felt a surge of triumphant courage rush along the pathways of her blood. With the release from panic, her brain began to function again, to count the odds, however slight.

There was something, the distance ventriloquist effect she had seen her father use effectively when there was sufficient space for it, the effect she had practiced but never had a chance to use herself. The distance from the living room door back to the kitchen area might be enough, barely enough. It was a tricky illusion requiring actual space, not imaginary. Still, its success would depend ultimately on her acting ability, whether she could make them believe in what she projected. She had to try. She must give David the opportunity he needed to take action.

As Tyron eyed her she let her lips part in dejected surrender. Her soft hazel eyes looked down, went alert, swept upward with surprise, peering into the dimness of the hallway past Tyron's shoulder to a spot not visible to anyone in the room and visible to Tyron only if he turned his attention away from her long enough to look.

Even if he thought she was mistaken, he dared not ignore the possibility that she had seen someone out there. After all, there had first been Linette.

He moved back, checking the hallway to be sure, and while his mind was momentarily misdirected, Petrina tightened her abdominal muscles and pushed her voice upward, outward, forcing resonance in her head cavity. She arched her tongue and pressed steadily upward from her diaphragm. Every nerve in her body was concentrated on projecting the illusion.

Her parted lips did not move. Tyron's hard eyes did not leave her face as he listened to a distant voice call shrilly, "Tell Joe and Ted to go get the sheriff. He's out there with Gordie—" Would David understand what she was doing?

With a curse Tyron swung his gun away from Petrina to cover the hallway just as David sprang and hit him. The Australian went smashing into the far wall, the gun flying from his hand and across the floor. At the same moment Catarina left her chair with an agility Petrina would not have believed possible and snatched the little wax doll from Morag's stiff fingers.

Ira's quickly retrieved shotgun bought them a measure of quiet as he marched Morag and the Australian back to the storeroom and bound them securely with a length of clothesline to the center post supporting the roof. Succinctly he reported when he returned, "Gagged them good, too. Needed to."

In the corner of the room Catarina finished a quiet ceremony she was performing over the ugly bit of wax in her hand. She stood up and carried it to a metal ashtray, sat the ashtray on the hearthstone of the fireplace, touched a match to the doll. It flared up with a startling flash and very quickly burned to ashes as she watched.

Petrina felt David's eyes on her and turned. "She said a prayer of purification over it," David said. "And she burned it." His thin face was white and drained. "Are you all right, Trina?"

The telephone rang as she started to speak and she went into the study to answer it. As she left the room David bent down and scooped Linette's limp body up in his arms and carried her upstairs, followed by Marinta and Sara to attend her.

In answer to the question she was asked on the telephone, Petrina gave directions, turn by turn, on how to reach the house from Cypress Glade. She replaced the instrument and suddenly, tears running down her cheeks, she began to laugh, close to hysteria.

David came down the stairs two at a time and ran to the study, shook her hard, once, twice.

"It was the man Julian sent," Petrina gasped. "And two men from the sheriff's office. And a man from Customs. All those people. There was a washout in the storm and they got lost on a detour. When all this happened they were that close, David."

He held her body against him until the paroxysm of reaction had worn itself out and then he led her down the hall, past the door of the living room, where Ira and Catarina sat somberly, silently looking at the body of Tony Addison lying on the floor under a shawl that Catarina had placed over him.

"The police will be here any minute," David said.

"*Sim.*" Catarina did not look up. "*Obrigado.*"

A breeze pushed down the hallway from the screened front door.

Outside the air was sweet and washed clean. A thin drizzle still fell but the clouds had thinned to a haze and there was no lightning.

David walked out into the damp darkness, stirring an earthy fragrance of wet vegetation as he moved. Petrina followed as though her feet would never know another path but his, not now, not ever. When they reached the seclusion of a shadowy cypress, he stopped and slowly turned to face her.

For a moment she stood motionless.

David's eyes touched her with hawklike intensity, moving over her, darkening suddenly as she trembled. She could feel the heat of him reaching out to her and her heart began to pound, almost suffocating her as she waited, half frightened, half exhilarated.

"Trina—" He spoke her name gently, so it was a light caress. "I love you. I desperately need you to love me too. Can you? Do you?"

He made no move toward her, his body held leashed by his will, his face pale. A pattern of light from the window caught an expression Panlike in its vitality and yearning on his face.

There had been other times when David Nairac had let down his guard with her enough to give her a glimpse of the blazing passions within him. But glimpses, swiftly hidden, were all she had ever known.

She began to understand why it had been like that as she stood before him, the mist cool against her face. Just as David had trained himself to keep a barrier between himself and the impinging thoughts of others, he had also trained himself to control and contain the vulnerability of his surging emotions.

Now as he opened his heart and emotions and thoughts to her it was like standing in an incandescent furnace, bathed in radiance, transmuted by inner flame that reached every nerve and cell in her body.

Her lips parted with the profound power of what she felt toward him in return and she ran toward him on feet that did not feel the ground beneath them. "David, I love you—"

His arms closed hard around her and with a soft cry

she melted against him, hearing the uneven thunder of his heartbeat before she raised her cheek from his chest, offering him her lips. His dark eyes held hers as his saturnine face bent closer. "You're sure, Trina? I'm not an easy man to care for, to live with—"

She felt the strength of his love begin to envelop her like a tide that could not be held back any longer. She did not answer, there was no need. The faint light from the window was blotted out as his lips crushed down against her mouth.

At the far end of the lane the headlights of a car turned toward the house and they could hear the sound of a motor approaching through air perfumed with a dreamlike fragrance of pine and the spring bloom of Spanish moss.

David raised his head without releasing her.

"It's almost over, David," Petrina whispered, her pulses throbbing, her nerves still tingling.

"Over?" David looked down again, smiling with tender amusement. His arms tightened. "No, it's not over, darling. It's only just beginning."